FORBIDDEN

FOREWARD
By Grace E. Watson, Reader and Avid Fan

★★★★★ Being raised in a Christian home, my siblings and I learned at a young age about the beginning of time, when God placed Adam and Eve in the Garden of Eden with instructions not to partake of the forbidden fruit. We knew that they couldn't resist the temptation, and as a result, sin was introduced into an otherwise perfect world. In her exciting, fictional book FORBIDDEN, Joan Fennell Carringer makes the creation come alive in vivid detail by taking the reader inside the hearts of the first man and woman. Then, through the lives of fictional characters in a modern day setting, she lets us see how vulnerable we all are and how we, too, are sometimes unable to resist the temptation of things that are forbidden – no matter how much they might hurt us and the ones we love. Using the familiar Word of God as a comparison to how the very first sin applies to our lives today, it is wonderfully written and inspiring to read, as well as a good refresher of God's everlasting love for us. I was drawn into this intriguing story from the very beginning and couldn't stop turning the pages until I'd finished it.

FORBIDDEN

An Inspirational Fiction Novel

BY
Joan Fennell Carringer

ONE

Her eyes flashing with eager anticipation, Danita began to write her story.

Eerie darkness and deathly silence were everywhere – in every corner, every nook and crevice, and every inch of space. In the air was a heaviness, a feeling of loneliness and dread, a frightful sensation of being forsaken and unwanted. It was certainly no place where any kind of life existed or could possibly ever come into being. Everything, everywhere was without form and void and darkness was upon the face of the deep.

Suddenly, there was a brilliant light shining through this place of darkness. Someone – or something - was there! The aura of intense power was running through this unseen presence, surrounding Him and everything close to Him. Who was He? Where did He come from? Why was He here in this strange place? What was He going to do? Did He see some possibility and hope in the midst of all the nothingness?

He stretched out His arms then and everything started changing! Light was everywhere. There was a blue sky, a dazzling sun and a moon, an ocean, green grass and trees. There were flat lands and mountains. There were animals, birds and creepy critters.

How could it possibly have happened that way? Danita stopped for a minute. It was pretty amazing, but it was also a little hard to believe, that anyone could be as powerful as the God of the Bible. She never was quite sure she believed it. Not that she didn't believe in God. She thought she did anyway, but for Him to have created heaven and earth in seven days? It was more like a fairy tale. How could it possibly have really, truly happened?   Oh, well, that wasn't for her to answer. All she had to do was write the story. Googling a few words that came to mind, she came across some scriptures, looked them up and went back to where she had left off.

In the beginning, GOD created the heaven and earth. Who was God and where did He come from? Was He simply always there? Did he come from everywhere but also from nowhere? The scripture clearly says that before the mountains were brought forth, before the earth and world were formed, from everlasting to everlasting, God was there. It also tells us that in the beginning was the Word, and the Word was with God, and the Word was God. The same was in the beginning with God. All things were made by Him; and without Him was not anything made that was made. In Him was life; and the life was the light of men.

Smiling at the thought, Danita's eyes became dreamy as she continued.

Beauty was now in the place of darkness. But still, even in the midst of it, God wasn't fully satisfied. He still felt alone. He didn't want it to be this way. He wanted something - besides the animals - who could provide real, true companionship and friendship, something He could have conversations with, something who favored Himself. None of the creatures did that.

As God skimmed his fingers through a handful of the dust from the ground, a brilliant idea came to Him. He knew exactly what He would do. Smiling from ear to ear, He envisioned it all. It would fulfill every desire within His heart and would be the beginning of something wonderful and everlasting. From that very same dust He would form His best creation ever – man. He would make him in His own image and give him breath from his own nostrils to make man become a living soul. Man would be His best friend. He would walk with Him and talk with Him and He would teach Him all the mysteries of life.

Danita stopped for a moment to think. So how would the first man and woman have felt when they suddenly came into being?

ADAM:

I opened my eyes and had to blink several times. Who was that staring back at me? Was it another being, such as I, or was it my own reflection? Was I looking into another's eyes or into a mirror? Who was I? What was I? Where had I come from? Until I took in a deep breath, I don't feel like I was anything at all. Now He's smiling and making me feel all jittery and tingly inside. It's almost like – like - He loves me – like I'm a part of Him – or like I wouldn't even be here if it wasn't for Him. What is going on? Maybe I'm not just seeing Him. Maybe I really am Him. But how can it be?   Now – oh, my goodness – now I feel like He's wanting me to speak to Him! But how can I, when I am so weak and He is so strong? I feel His power surging through the depth of myself, from His eyes still staring at me, from His hands touching me, from everywhere inside of Him to everything inside of myself!   What a wondrous sensation!

I quickly learn that this being is my Creator, His name is God, and He tells me I am called man. We walk together in this beautiful garden. It's indescribable here and I love it. But something seems to be going on in the mind of God and finally I find out what it is. He doesn't want me to be alone. He is going to make me a helpmeet. I wonder what it will be like. Will it look like me? Then there will be three in the same image – God, me and my helpmeet. I can hardly wait.....

And the Lord God caused a deep sleep to fall upon Adam, and he slept; and He took one of his ribs, and closed up the flesh instead thereof: And the rib, which the Lord God had taken from the man, made he a woman, and brought her unto the man.

ADAM:

Gosh! I must have fallen asleep. When I first saw her, I thought I must be dreaming. How could anything be so beautiful? She doesn't look anything like God or me! She's smaller and her skin is softer and so creamy and smooth. Her hair is shiny and long, falling in long curls over her slender shoulders. But what shall I call her? Woman! I will call her woman because she was taken out of man. But her name will be Eve. Yes, I like that name, and I am sure I am going to like this new strange creature God has given to me!

EVE:

Adam and I are so very happy living in this beautiful garden. We have everything we could ever want or need. The best part of it all is that we can stay forever, living in perfect peace and harmony – as long as we don't eat fruit from one particular tree. I don't think that's too much to ask. After all, God is so good to us and all He asks is that we stay away from that forbidden fruit. He has to have a reason. Maybe it will make us sick if we eat it. Whatever being sick is. I have no idea. God says we will die if we eat it, but I don't know what that means either because I don't know what it means to die. All I have ever done is live.

I met something odd today. It is called a serpent and if I knew the definition of ugly, that's how I would describe it. It certainly does not favor either Adam or me and it has to slither around on the ground because it doesn't have strong legs like we do. But it talks to me and its mind seems very wise. It just told me that the forbidden fruit is the most delicious of anything else in the garden and we won't die if we eat it. It says we will become better people instead and we will understand the difference in good and evil. I don't know about evil. I have never seen it, only good things. But it might be helpful to know what it was, so I wouldn't ever become trapped in its clutches. God would surely understand and accept that reasoning. I'm thinking about what the serpent told me. In fact, I can't stop thinking about it. The serpent is very convincing.

I look at that tree and the fruit and the longer my eyes rest on it, the more beautiful and enticing it becomes. I want it so badly! I can almost taste it on my tongue. I reach my hand out and touch it, but then I pull away. God said I shouldn't. But it must be so delicious. Maybe that's why God doesn't want me to eat it, because it tastes so much better than anything else and He's afraid it's all I'll want from now on and all the other fruit wouldn't ever be eaten. I smiled. That surely wouldn't happen. All I would do is take one tiny, little bite. Then my curiosity would be satisfied. God would never even have to know! I grabbed it before I could change my mind. I bit into it.

Adam is coming and he's seen me, so I hold it out to him and beg him to taste it, too. He does, and we laugh. But then something very strange happens. We look at each other and are overcome with embarrassment to realize we are totally naked. Why did we never know this before? We decide to entwine some fig leaves together and cover our bodies. That would surely work.

But now God is coming and He doesn't look happy at all. Could He possibly know what we've done? For the first time in my life, I feel fear. I am afraid of God. What is He going to do?

GOD, watching Adam and Eve leaving the Garden of Eden forever:

I never wanted this to happen. I had to make them leave, even though I dearly love the man and woman I created. It was because of my love for them that I gave them their own free will, allowing them to make their own choices. I wanted their obedience because they truly loved Me in their hearts, not because I forced it on them. The evil serpent knew this and took full advantage of it. He will go into the outside world with them and cause them trouble for as long as they live, for as long as their future generations live. But I have worked out the perfect plan of salvation – and everything will not be lost. My loved ones and I will not be separated forever. My absolutely perfect plan cannot fail......

TWO

DANITA SIGHED AND LOOKED AWAY from her story. Running her hands through her long blonde hair, she couldn't suppress a yawn. That led to her blue eyes starting to water, and pushing her reading glasses up onto her forehead, she rubbed them gently. How long had she been sitting at this computer? She'd been so deeply engrossed in studying the creation in the Bible and trying to imagine how the first two people must have felt that time had flown by like minutes. Looking at the clock, she was surprised to see that it had been hours instead.

Her thoughts returned to Adam and Eve. Eve had brought on a lot of trouble and chaos to the rest of the world because of her rebellious decision to have what she wanted. Then again, why did God strictly forbid her and Adam to eat of that particular fruit? If the truth were known, it probably didn't taste any differently than anything else growing in the garden. It may not have looked any better either. Physically, that is. Its real appeal was probably simply due to the fact that it was forbidden. Aren't we all more attracted to what we can't have than what we can? As far as that goes, there isn't much of anything that's fun if it isn't forbidden in one way or another.

She quickly stopped her thoughts. She didn't want to go there. She couldn't go there.

The only thing she had to do was transpose some of the most popular Bible stories into something more people would understand and enjoy reading. Something more interesting. Something fun. But where in the world did fun have any place in the story of Adam and Eve? Certainly not when they were kicked out of Paradise because of one little mistake.

It wasn't just a mistake, her conscience retaliated. It was a direct defiance to God.

Still.....if it hadn't happened, would anyone else ever have been born? Her eyes widened. Then she smiled at the thought and her imagination ran on once again.

ADAM AND EVE

"Are you crying?" Adam asked his wife as they walked together.

"I am afraid. Aren't you?"

"God had every right to do what He did. He told you over and over not to touch that forbidden fruit."

Her eyes flashed. "Me? You're blaming it all on me? You ate it, too."

"You gave it to me."

"I didn't force you to eat it."

"It doesn't matter. You already had the first bite so the damage was already done."

"But it wasn't all my fault. It was that....that ugly creature, whatever it was. It could've told me anything and I would've believed it."

"Then why wouldn't you listen to God when He told you not to eat it? I'd think God should be obeyed before some unknown, slivering serpent."

"When God pointed out the tree, I wasn't tempted in the least by it. It never entered my mind that the fruit would taste any differently than any of the others, but when the thing asked me to look at it, it looked – well, it looked prettier and fresher and so much tastier. It's like I saw it one way through God's eyes and another way through the eyes of the serpent."

Adam didn't answer but walked on, wiping perspiration from his brow as he did. He'd never been uncomfortable before and now he was feeling much too warm. Not only that, he was tired walking and wanting to do nothing but lie down and sleep. He'd never been tired before.   Stopping for a moment, he took in a deep breath.

"Why are you stopping?" she wanted to know.

"I'm tired. We need to sleep." He sat down on the ground, propping his back against a tree trunk. "Oh, this ground is hard!" He shifted positions.

She didn't sit beside him but merely stood there watching him.

He raised his eyes. "Aren't you tired?"

She smiled and her eyes sparkled. "I think I'll just stand here and look at you."

"What a silly thing to say. Why would you want to do that?"

"I like the way you look. Remember how God told us we'll have children?"

"I remember. I also remember He said it would multiply our sorrow."

"But I'm thinking of something else, something more pleasurable."

He looked at her with questioning eyes.

"The conception of our children."

"What about it?"

"Adam, I know what you look like."

"And I know what you look like. What does that have to do with anything?"

"I mean, before we had to be clothed, I have seen your anatomy."

"And I have seen your anatomy."

"We are different."

"I know."

She sat down then, very close to him. "I don't think we should worry about having children, not for a while anyway. If God really wants it to happen, He will see that it is done. But, in the meantime, while we are waiting, I think…." She grinned at him and edged even closer, putting her hand upon his chest and running it around and around. "Well, I think, it might be enjoyable to……"

"To what?" Suddenly his eyes widened. "You mean, we should…..?"

She kept smiling.

Reaching out to her, he pulled her into his arms. Maybe something good would come from their being exiled after all. At the moment, it certainly felt good to be so close to such a beautiful creature. He'd worry about their future problems later.

THREE

JAMES WALKED INTO THE ROOM quietly and smiled at his wife. So many times, he had come home to find Danita reared back in the recliner next to her computer, sound asleep. She was so beautiful. No wonder he was still as crazy about her as he was on their wedding day ten years ago. If anything, he loved her even more now than he did then.

But did she still feel the same way about him? He tried not to let himself think about it, but he was doing that very thing more and more lately. He knew she had to spend a lot of time on the stories she wrote as a freelancer, and he tried not to be jealous of the hours she spent at the computer that could've been their together time instead. She enjoyed what she did and he was happy for her, but was she taking on more and more jobs lately or was it his imagination? She didn't have to work. They didn't need the money. He made a very good living for them in his computer business. Truth be told, they had more in their savings than a lot of people ever earned. Of course, it required him to be gone a lot and he knew she needed something to fill the hours without him, but still it bothered him that they were seeing less and less of each other. When he suggested going on a vacation, he thought she'd be pleased and excited. Instead, she told him she was working on a deadline and the vacation would have to wait. She never said for how long. She just never mentioned it again.

Nearly every evening, he found her asleep in her office. He did the same thing each time, woke her gently and led her to the bedroom. The minute her head hit the pillow, she was asleep again.

With a sigh, he looked at her computer screen. Sometimes she'd ask him if he wanted to read her latest story but most times she wrote them, turned them in and never said anything about them. Bringing the screen to life, he looked at the last words on the page in front of him.

Reaching out to her, he pulled her into his arms. Maybe something good would come from their being exiled after all. At the moment, it certainly felt good to be so close to such a beautiful creature. He'd worry about their future problems later.

His dark eyebrows furrowed together. When had she started writing love stories? He raised his eyes to scan over some of the preceding paragraphs. Oh, yes! This was the story about Adam and Eve. She was doing a special series on the Bible characters, trying to make them real and human in the eyes of the reader.

He yawned and ran his hands through his short dark wavy hair. As he did, he glanced at the clock. Midnight. No wonder she fell asleep before he got home. He had to quit working so many late hours.

He tapped her gently on the shoulder. "Dani. Wake up, honey."

She jumped, startled, but then sat up straight and smiled at him. "I did it again." She yawned. "What time is it?"

"Bedtime. I'm sorry I was so late."

"It's okay. I had lots of time to get this story going."

It wasn't the answer he wanted. How long had it been since she'd told him she missed him when he was working so many hours?

She stood up.

"I read a little of the last part. Are you going to give Adam and Eve a steamy relationship?"

"Not hardly. This is for a Christian magazine. That little bit is just enough to keep the reader's interest, to make them remember they are man and wife and they're destined to have children. I mean, if they hadn't, where would we be?"

"I know where I'd like to be, on a big long vacation with my beautiful wife. Have you given it any more thought? When will you have some free time?"

"I have quite a few deadlines right now, James."

"But why? You started doing this to fill in some time but now it's taking all your time. And ours."

"You should talk. What time is it?" She looked at the clock. "Midnight. Again."

"Would it make any difference if I came home at five or six? You'd be awake but you'd still be here working."

"I'm tired. I'm going to bed."

He put his arm around her but she pulled away. With a sigh, he started out of the room without her.

He couldn't sleep. Lying beside the woman he loved, he listened to her soft, even breathing. She wouldn't awaken until after he was already up and gone to work again. Tomorrow would be the same as today and the day after and the day after.

What could he do to make things better? He'd leave her a note on the table, telling her he wanted to take her to dinner and dancing. She loved to dance and it had been forever since they'd gone out. There was no way she could turn down that invitation. Maybe he'd suggest she ask her best friend Liz and her husband Tom if they wanted to come with them. They used to have such great times together but it had been a long time.

As he made plans in his mind, he saw her all dressed up in one of her many beautiful gowns, twirling around in front of him the way she used to do, laughing and joking. He saw them together in the restaurant and felt the envy of other men when they looked at her. He always loved that. She was his and he was proud of it. He was proud of her.

DANI pretended to sleep, just as she often did lately. If he knew she was awake, he'd want to talk and that would lead to – other things. She just didn't want to keep turning him down, so the easiest thing to do was fain sleep.

When had she started feeling this way? She had loved him when she married him and she still loved him. They were happy and had a lot of good times together. He was good to her and they rarely argued about anything.

Her mind returned to the story she was writing. Had Adam and Eve truly and passionately loved each other? There was no one else for either of them to compare the other with. They were the only people on earth. How could they know for sure?

She knew exactly when she'd started feeling as she did, the moment she'd seen Max again and started comparing him and her husband.

Max. Tall, blonde, blue-eyed and deliciously handsome. She dated him before she met James, when she was only seventeen, and was sure she was head over heels in love with him. But Max wasn't wanting a serious relationship with anyone and less than a year later, he left her for someone else.

He moved away and she didn't see him again until a month ago. Suddenly, there he was, in the same parking lot, his pickup truck parked right beside her car. They started talking, lightly at first, but then he told her he'd made the worst mistake of his life when he left her.

She sighed, immediately regretting her action when her husband leaned over and kissed her cheek.

"You okay?"

"I – must have been dreaming. I'm fine." Rolling over, she closed her eyes again, hoping James would quickly fall asleep.

He did.   At least she thought he did, but mostly she thought of Max. He'd wished her well. He told her he was happy about her marriage, that he knew James and knew he'd be good to her.

She'd been happy with James before that meeting. Now all she felt was confusion. Every time she thought of James, she found herself also thinking of Max. What was wrong with her? She'd been so deeply in love with Max, but she was also deeply in love with her husband. It was almost as if she was in love with both of them.

She didn't expect to start thinking again of the story she was writing about Adam and Eve. When Eve had everything she could ever want or need to make her happy, all she wanted was the one thing that she couldn't have. That one forbidden fruit.

Was she a lot more like Eve than she knew?

Eve gave in – and sin took over the world.

That was then and this is now, Dani thought, defending her desire for another man other than her husband.

Eve disobeyed God.

Wasn't her marriage sacred in God's eyes? Didn't she make a promise, before Him, to stay with James until death parted them?

"I don't want to think about this," she thought quietly. "I want to go to sleep, wake up and be madly in love with James and only James. But right now, the one I want the most is – Max."

Just as all Eve wanted was to eat the fruit.

FOUR

SHE WIPED HER EYES, her heart a mixture of both sadness and anger. How could he be so sweet all the time? Crumbling the note in her hand, she threw it into the trashcan and picked up her cup of coffee. Just when she'd finally decided to talk to him about her true feelings, he wanted to go out to dinner and dancing. And even invite her best friends along. Maybe she should do it. Shouldn't she at least try to recapture some of the good times before she gave up completely?

What if Max found someone else in the meantime? She hated the thought, but mostly she hated herself for thinking it. Why couldn't she put him out of her mind? Why couldn't she dwell on how happy she'd been in her marriage with James, a man who loved her with every fiber of his being, instead of on the man who had broken her heart?

Did Eve have this same feeling of dissatisfaction? Was the real reason she took that one forbidden bite because she wanted it, not because the serpent told her it wouldn't kill her and would make her smarter instead, but because she had a void in her heart that she needed to satisfy? Maybe it had nothing at all to do with the enticing beauty of the fruit. Maybe it didn't matter what the tempter told her. Maybe she wasn't satisfied with her life and just had to try something different.

"What am I going to do, keep trying to analyze Eve's life or live my own?" Danita spoke the words aloud in a voice of anger. "Why does it matter why she did what she did? There's no way to change anything. That is, if all this really even happened. Maybe the Bible's just a big book of fairy-tales, like I used to read when I was a kid. There are so many incredible, unbelievable stories. Noah building that big ark. Jonah being swallowed by a whale."

She stopped when the phone rang and picked it up quickly, glad for a distraction to her thoughts.

Wrong number. Wouldn't you know?

She needed to get her story submitted. As she started toward her home office, she stopped short when a flash of something through the window caught her eye. What was it? For just a split second, she was sure someone was out there but it passed so quickly she couldn't be sure of it. Her heart began to race. Had someone been watching her? Had he turned away the moment he thought she might see him?

She stood very still, waiting, and continuing to stare out the window. Even as she watched, never blinking an eye, she expected the doorbell to ring, but it never did. Had it all been her imagination? Finally, after a long sigh, she turned and finished her trek to her home office.

She jumped when the phone rang again, shattering the stillness. Another wrong number?

"I just wanted to say good morning." It was her husband.

"Good morning, James."

"Did you get my note? Do you want me to go ahead and make some reservations for dinner tonight?"

"I haven't talked to Liz yet. They might not be able to go."

He laughed. "It's okay. I talked to Tom just a few minutes ago and he thought it was a wonderful idea."

"You talked to him before you even talked to me? You're jumping the gun a little, don't you think? What if I can't get away this evening? You know what a deadline I've been under."

"I also know you're working too much and need a little reprieve. It'll be fun, honey."

She sighed. As she did, she raised her eyes toward the window and became startled. It happened again! It was like someone had walked by, just like the other time, but it happened so fast.   It was like a flash, gone too quickly to tell what it was. She kept watching, unable to take her eyes away and didn't reply to her husband's last words.

"Dani? You still there? You aren't upset that I talked to Tom, are you? I mean, I didn't jump the gun, as you stated. I left you a note. I figured it was okay when you didn't call back."

"I didn't have time to call back. I just saw the note." Her eyes were still on the window. Should she say something to James?

He chuckled. "Guess you slept in, huh? Its okay, honey. You needed the rest."

"I need to go. If I actually get away this evening, I have a lot to do. One story to submit, another to start."

"I'll be home by five. I'll make the reservations for seven, so we'll have plenty of time to get ready."

She certainly didn't need two hours to get ready. Didn't he know that by now? "Okay, I'll see you then."

"Bye, honey. Love you."

"Bye." She hung up the phone, surprised to find tears brimming in her eyes. Why hadn't she said I love you back to him, the way she always had before? What was wrong with her? He was the perfect husband. No woman could ask for a better man. He was not only handsome, he was a good Christian and he'd probably never done a bad deed in his life.

She remembered him telling her that he'd gone through a wild stage when he was young, but he never went into detail. Didn't all boys do that? Knowing James, he probably felt condemned if he stayed out past his curfew. Maybe he went over the speed limit a little too often.

She couldn't suppress a grin. There was no way he could've ever done anything really bad. It wasn't in him now and couldn't have been then.

He would certainly never spend his time fantasizing about a former lover. If he ever stopped loving her, he would be honest enough to tell her.

She wanted to slap herself for the thought, but just the same, she believed it was true.

Maybe if he was younger or she was older it would be different. She was twenty-nine and he was thirty-eight. She recalled how his maturity had been one of her main attractions to him. She didn't want to marry a boy. She wanted a man, and he was certainly that. But that was ten years ago. When she was nineteen and he was still in his twenties, the age difference didn't seem to matter at all. Not even when he hit thirty, two years after they were married did it make any difference.

She knew in her heart that it had all started the day she saw Max again. Max, with his thick wavy blonde hair without a strain of grey and sparkling blue eyes filled with laughter. She couldn't help comparing those eyes to the age beginning to show in her husbands and thinking of how James' dark hair was suddenly streaked with grey. And James was tired a lot. Max was still filled with vitality.

She had to change her train of thought.

Her mind returned to what she'd thought she saw at the window. Not once, but twice and at two different windows. Maybe she should go outside and look around.

She told herself she needed to stay exactly where she was and start working. Truthfully, she didn't have nearly as much to do as she'd let on. Lately, her work had just been a quick excuse for getting out of other things she didn't want to do.

Like spending more time with her husband.

FIVE

LIZ LAUGHED AND EVERYONE LAUGHED WITH HER. She was so delightful, always happy and upbeat, and even though she was Dani's best friend, Dani couldn't help feeling a twinge of envy.   She had never seen Liz in a bad or sad mood. She was always perfectly content, no matter what happened. And she was so much in love with her husband Tom. Turning her eyes toward him, Dani couldn't miss the open adoration he had for his wife. That he loved her and adored her was clearly apparent, from the way he seemed to watch every move she made to how he gently ran his fingers up and down her arm, to the loving way he was continually smiling into her eyes or kissing her cheek.

Liz openly returned his feelings. No doubt about it, they were the perfect couple. Not only were they happy, they were also gorgeous. Liz, with her short dark hair and dark brown eyes and Tom, blonde-haired and blue-eyed were so different in looks, yet at the same time, so strikingly beautiful together. They were truly a match made in heaven.

Which one would their baby look like? In just two more months, their first child would be born and it seemed to be all they wanted to talk about. They would be such wonderful parents.

Dani's mind stopped when she felt her own husband's gaze on her and she turned toward him. At the sight of the love shining in his eyes, guilt immediately surged through her. She forced herself to smile back at him sweetly, hoping he couldn't see the pretense behind her action.

He stood up and held out his arms without saying a word. With her fake smile still on her lips, she stood up also and accepted his hand, then followed him onto the dance floor.

A slow number was playing and she leaned her face against his chest as they moved perfectly to the rhythm of the music. She used to feel shivers running all through her body when he held her that way. His slightest touch would start all her senses roaring with excitement.

"Penny for your thoughts," he whispered.

She forced a chuckle. "You wouldn't get your money's worth, believe me."

"Did I mention how lovely you look this evening, honey? I love the way you have all that golden blonde hair piled on top of your head and that deep blue dress really makes your eyes sparkle."

She didn't reply.

"Liz sure looks comical, doesn't she?"

"Comical?"

"Comical, but cute. She's as round as she is short. Have you noticed how she waddles when she walks?"

Dani's laugh was genuine this time. "I've noticed."

"I've noticed something else, too. She has a glow around her. She's twice as lovely as she was before she got pregnant."

"She's always been beautiful. I've always envied her creamy smooth skin."

"Honey, she doesn't have a thing that you need to envy, believe me."

They were silent for a few minutes as the music continued before James spoke again. "You know what?"

"What?"

"Maybe we should think about starting a family."

Her heart flinched and she didn't answer. With all the mixed emotions swirling around inside her, it was the last thing she wanted to talk about.

"We talked about it, you know, when we first got married. We agreed to wait until we felt like we were financially able to take care of children. Well, we are now. I have a great job and you don't have to work unless you want to. We have a beautiful home with a big yard and a huge wooded acre behind it. We own a kids' paradise, but there are no kids to enjoy it."

Paradise. Adam and Eve lived in paradise, but it all ended and they wound up with nothing.

When she didn't answer him, he kissed the top of her head. "Will you think about it? I'm not only ready, I'm not getting any younger, you know."

The music stopped and she was relieved that she didn't have to say anything else as he led her back to their table. Once there, Tom started a new conversation and everyone joined in, talking, laughing and enjoying being together.

In the lighter atmosphere, Dani found herself feeling increasingly happier and eager to join in the laughter that surrounded the table of friends.

Until she raised her eyes and saw Max. She almost gasped aloud. Never in a million years did she expect to see him there. He'd never liked this kind of place. When they were dating, he'd made fun of them, calling them the rich man's paradise where men and women went to show off their expensive clothing and jewelry. Now, here he was. Not only that, he was dressed in an immaculate blue suit and shiny black shoes. The kind of clothes he used to make jokes about.

All her thoughts stopped when she realized he was looking straight at her and walking toward her. What was he doing? What would her husband think? She remembered that James would have no idea who Max was. She'd never mentioned him, not once in all their years together. Max had shattered her heart in so many pieces that she never spoke of him to anyone.

But Liz had been her friend even then and she knew who he was. Turning, Dani met Liz' eyes and clearly saw the confusion within them as she looked from Dani to Max then back to Dani.

Neither James nor Tom, still deep in conversation, noticed what was happening around them. They only stopped talking when Max approached the table and spoke.

"Dani and Liz! What a surprise. I haven't seen either of you in years."

Dani swallowed, having no idea what to say

Liz merely smiled. "Hello, Max. I didn't know you were back in town."

Tom and James looked quizzically, first at Liz, then at Dani, then at Max.

Dani found her voice. Forcing a smile, she said, "James, this is Max Baker. He and I – and Liz – were friends when we were teen agers. Max, my husband James Starrman, and Liz's husband Tom Grant."   Upon impulse, she touched her husband's arm lovingly as she spoke.

Both James and Tom stood up and shook Max's hand.

"So nice to meet you, Max," Tom said, smiling. "I guess if you were friends with my wife and Dani when you were teen agers, you probably have some funny tales to tale, huh?"

James merely said, "Nice to meet you, Max. Would you like to join us?"

Max' blue eyes twinkled. "Oh, no, I'm with someone. I just saw Dani and Liz and had to come by and say hello." He looked first at Liz, then at Dani. "Would either of you beautiful ladies like to share a dance with me, for old times' sake?"

Dani's heart began to race at the mere thought of being in Max's arms. Memories raced through her mind of how it used to be with them, all the hugs and the kisses, the whispered words of love and the promises that they would always be together.

Tom's laughter broke her train of thought. "I guess it will have to be Dani, Max." Gently, he pulled his very pregnant wife to her feet. "My wife doesn't do much dancing anymore."

Max grinned, then looked at Dani. "Dani?"

Dani looked at her husband. "James......"

James smiled. "Go ahead, honey. One dance for old times' sake never hurt anyone."

What could she do but follow Max across the floor and go into his open arms? The minute their bodies touched, a surge of emotions ran through her - warm, exotic feelings that she could no more stop them than she could stop breathing.

"You are the most beautiful woman in this room," he whispered into her ear.

She had to control herself! When she spoke, her voice was surprisingly calm. "What about the one you're with? You said you were with someone."

"She's okay. Just a friend. I've never found anybody else to replace you. Not even when I was married."

Married.   She didn't reply but waited for him to continue.

"We tried for five years and decided it wasn't worth it."

"Kids?"

"No, thank goodness. I hate getting them involved in a divorce. I never want kids."

James' words ran through her mind, about his longing to start a family.

Max pulled her closer and kissed her forehead. "Ohh, it's been too long for you and me!"

She had to get away from him, her mind cried out in warning, but her body refused to move. "Don't say that," she breathed. "Just don't say it."

"What's wrong? Honey, you're trembling. You act like you're scared of me."

"I'm not scared of you."

"Well, I'm scared of you."

"What are you talking about?"

"I'm scared that since you're in my arms again, I won't be able to let you go."

Her heart raced even faster and she said nothing.

"Do you want me to let you go? Do you love him?"

"He's my husband."

"That's not what I asked you."

"Of course I love him."

"I think you're lying. I think you still love me and I know I still love you."

"Then why did you leave me?"

"I was a fool."

She didn't reply. She couldn't say another word because she knew if she did, she'd start to cry. Not only would she embarrass herself but she'd also prove to Max that what he was saying was true. Would he want her to leave James? Or would he try to convince her they could just have an affair, and James would never have to know?

And why, oh why, was she so reluctant to even consider what her answer would be if he suggested it?

"He's a little old for you, don't you think?"

She couldn't listen to anymore. Pushing him away forcefully, she walked back to the table, told James she needed to take a quick trip to the ladies' room and left again quickly.

She wasn't surprised when Liz followed her. "Did you know he was back?"

Dani shook her head. "I saw him one time, about a month ago, in the parking lot when I was buying groceries. We talked. That was all, Liz. We merely talked."

"I think you talked just now, too. You are visibly shaken. What did he say to you?"

Dani didn't answer but merely stared at her reflection in the mirror.

Liz spoke softly. "James is a wonderful man, Dani, and he loves you with all his heart. He would never hurt you. Max nearly caused you to have a nervous breakdown once and I'm not convinced that he wouldn't do it again if he had the chance."

Anger flashed in Dani's eyes. "For goodness sake, all we did was dance!"

"What did he say to you?"

"Nothing."

"I know when you're lying."

Dani turned and her blue eyes met forcefully with Liz's brown ones. For a long moment they stared at each other, neither saying a word.

It was Liz who pulled away first. "I'll be praying for you. I believe you're already in trouble and don't even know it." She gave Dani a quick hug. "I love you." Turning away, she walked across the floor, opened the door and left the room.

Dani stood still for a long time, thinking of her friend's words. 'I'll be praying for you. I believe you're already in trouble and don't even know it.'

"You're wrong," she whispered. "Prayer won't help me, because I don't just think I'm in trouble. I know I am. And prayer won't help."

Did Eve pray before she took that forbidden bite? Would it have made any difference if she had?

SIX

JAMES' EYES WIDENED IN SURPRISE when he opened the coffee canister the next morning. He knew it had been full the day before and now there was hardly any left. What had happened to it? Dani couldn't be drinking that much coffee while she worked on her computer. If she was, she had better slow down if she wanted to avoid some severe health problems.

Pushing it to the back of his mind, he started what coffee he had brewing and fixed himself a bowl of cereal. But when he opened the refrigerator to get the milk and saw that it, too, was nearly empty, just like the coffee can, he shook his head in disbelief. For a while, he merely stared at it, wondering if his eyes were playing tricks on him. He was certain there had been plenty of both coffee and milk the day before. Hadn't there? Or was he losing his mind or something? With a sigh, he used what milk was available and sat down at the table to eat the bowl of nearly dry cereal.

To his surprise, his wife walked into the kitchen. It was unusual for her to be up before he left for work. Everything else left his mind as he smiled at her. Even with her hair rumpled from sleep and wearing an old worn robe and slippers, she was the most beautiful woman he had ever seen. "Good morning. I didn't expect to see you up so early."

She yawned and went to the coffee pot. "I didn't sleep well, so I decided I may as get up and start the day. Only a half pot of coffee today, James? How long have you been here drinking it?" She smiled wryly at her husband as she sat beside him at the table.

Leaning over, he kissed her forehead. "There was only enough coffee to make half a pot. Not only that, the milk is gone, too."

Her eyes widened. "But I just bought milk two days ago and the coffee can was full yesterday."

"I know. So where did it go?"

"Your guess is as good as mine. I never drink milk, can't stand it. You know that, but coffee, well that's something I have to have." She took a sip.

He sighed. "Maybe we have our days mixed up. Maybe it was longer ago than we remember that we replaced them. Time goes so fast, I can't keep up with it anymore."

She didn't answer as she continued to sip her coffee. She was certain it had only been two days since she'd bought the milk and there was plenty of coffee.

"I have to go out of town again," he said then. "I'll have to leave this evening, so could you have my bag packed for me when I get home? There's an early morning meeting tomorrow for the set up and programming of a huge computer system in Atlanta."

"Sure."

"Sure?"

"I'll have your bag ready for you. Should I fix dinner?"

"No, I'll bring something home. What would you like?"

"It doesn't matter."

"You sound a little down. Are you okay?"

"I'm fine, just tired. I told you, I didn't sleep well."

He grinned. "I slept like a baby. We had such a great time together last night and I went to bed as happy as I could be. Sleep came easy. Sorry, it wasn't like that for you." He stood up. "I need to go. Let's have a little prayer first, okay?"

She nodded, took the hand he offered and bowed her head. James always did this, prayed before he left the house. She usually wasn't there to join him, but she was sure he did it alone, too.   His words were soft, yet meaningful as he asked the Heavenly Father to guide and direct their day and keep them safe. She loved the sound of his voice. It was soothing and gentle. She was glad she'd gotten there before he left.

When he finished, he bent over and kissed her lips lightly. "I love you."

"Love you, too."

As she watched him leave, her heart hurt. He was such a good man and a devoted Christian. He'd meant every word he'd just said, especially when he told her he loved her. She'd said the words because he expected her to, but did she mean them as much as he did?

She decided she wasn't going to dwell on the question. Picking up her coffee cup, she drank what was left of it and went to take a shower. Afterward, feeling refreshed and much better, she went to her home office and booted up her computer.

The sunshine streaming through the window caught her attention, instead of working, she sat staring at it. She didn't want to be sitting in front of a computer. She wanted to be outside. Even if she did nothing but walk around, she wanted to be out there feeling the warmth of the fresh spring air surging through her body.

A vision popped into her mind. Two young people, sitting on the bank fishing. Laughing, talking. Stopping every few minutes to steal a kiss. Then they were in the water, swimming, bobbing up and down, playing splash games – and always winding up in each other's arms. It was her and Max.

They had been so much in love. Or so she thought. They'd both been too young. He was the only one smart enough to know it.

She stood up, willing her mind to stop. She was going to make herself forget him. She had a wonderful husband, a beautiful home and everything she could ever want. Max Baker had shattered her life one time. Once was enough. She wasn't going to let him do it again. Her heart wasn't the only one involved this time. There was also James.

After trying to work but finding it impossible to concentrate, she stood up again. She had to get outside, if just for a little while. She needed some fresh air, but first she needed some coffee. Not until she got to the kitchen did she remember there wasn't any. Maybe she should go to the store. She'd have to go before morning for sure. Neither James nor she could get by without that early caffeine fix. But James wouldn't be there in the morning. At the remembrance, she felt a tug at her heart. She was going to miss him.

The thought surprised her, but made her happy all at the same time. It was true. She loved her husband. Why, then, did she have such mixed feelings and raging emotions for

Max? She recalled the way it felt to be in his arms the night before. It was as if the last ten years had never happened, that she and Max were still 17 and 18 and madly in love. Was that what it was, a craving for the past, a desire to once again be young and free?

Or was she more like Eve than she knew? Did she want her former love in the same way Eve had craved that piece of fruit? Was one forbidden object – or person – the same as another? What would she have done if she'd been Eve? What was she going to do now?

She sat down on the porch swing and looked around her. All the trees were budding out and the grass was so fresh and green. What a beautiful time of the year. Maybe if she put her mind entirely upon the beauty and splendor of the creation, she'd be able to rid herself of her frustrations.

She thought of how she loved her home. It was an old house, owned by James' parents and given to him, since he was an only child, when they decided they couldn't keep it up anymore and wanted a smaller place. He'd worked on remodeling before he and Dani were married and afterward, they'd finished it together, making it exactly the way they wanted it.

Her thoughts stopped abruptly when she saw a car slowing down and then turning into the driveway. Liz. A smile crossed her lips at the thoughts of spending some more time with her best friend, until she remembered their words the night before. No doubt Liz had come to give her a good chewing out. Maybe she needed to talk about it. Maybe it would clear her head of some of the things she was suddenly so disturbed about.

When Liz seemed to be having trouble getting out of the car, Dani went to help her. "If you get much bigger, you're going to have to buy a bus," she teased.

"I sure will be glad when this baby is born. I feel like I weigh a ton. Now don't you dare say I look like it, too." Liz laughed.

So did Dani. "All kidding aside, are you feeling okay, other than the weight?"

"I do. Honestly, I feel great."

Dani took her hand and they walked together onto the porch, then sat down side by side on the glider. "Want something to drink?"

Liz reached into her bag and pulled out a bottle of water. "This is all my liquid refreshment right now." Removing the lid, she took a big swallow and then replaced it.

"That reminds me. The strangest thing happened this morning. James went to make the coffee and the canister was nearly empty. We're both certain it was full yesterday. Then he went to get some milk for his cereal and it was nearly all gone. I bought milk just a couple days ago and it always lasts us a couple weeks. We can't figure out what happened to them."

"Hmm. That's strange. You're sure you had lots or did the time get away from you and you just thought you had?"

"That's what James said, but it still puzzles me. It's like we've had a coffee and milk thief."

Liz laughed. "So somebody must really be craving coffee and milk. Come on, Dani. The time got away from you, like I just said, and you know it. Now....about Max Baker."

Dani sighed. "I figured that's why you came by."

"We need to talk about this."

"There's nothing to talk about."

"You were really shook up after that dance. I'm surprised James didn't notice. He doesn't know about Max, does he?"

"I never told him."

"Why not?"

"Why should I? Max wasn't my only boyfriend before James and I met and I'm sure I wasn't James' only girlfriend."

"But Max is the only one you loved. I was really scared for you when he left you. I was afraid you'd think about suicide or something, as depressed as you were."

"I'm too big a coward to kill myself. I'm too scared about what I'd find on the other side."

"I've always been unsettled as to whether a person can go to heaven if he takes his own life. I mean, the Bible clearly says 'Thou shalt not kill'. If you take your own life, it's even worse than killing someone else because you never have a chance to be really sorry and ask for forgiveness."

"This is kind of morbid, so let's change the subject, okay? Isn't it the perfect, beautiful day?"

"Yes, but I was still surprised to see you sitting out here on the porch. I figured you'd be hard at work on the computer."

"I need to be, but I couldn't concentrate. I'll work tonight. James has to go to Atlanta, so I'll be all alone and, hopefully, I'll finish up my assignment."

"How long does he have to stay in Atlanta?"

"He didn't say, but they're getting into a really big job there."

"It seems like all either of you two do is work. You need to slow down, stop and smell the roses."

Dani chuckled. "It's too early in the spring. They aren't out yet."

"So – about Max?"

"We already talked about him. There's nothing more to say."

"I think there is. Out with it."

Dani sighed. "I get emotional when he's around."

"And?"

"And – that's all."

"There's nothing more than that between you?"

Dani said nothing.

"Dani?"

"It scares me, because all the memories come raging back of how it was with us – when it was good."

"And how long was that? Six months?"

"We went together for a year."

"If I remember correctly, you were only contented with each other for about six months."

"That's not true. Oh, there were times....."

"Lots of times. I know because you came crying to me quite often. Okay, I know you don't want to hear that. So, you went together for a year. Even if the entire year was good, which I know it wasn't, you can't compare that one year to the ten years you've had with James. Don't let yourself even think about it. It can only cause trouble."

"How do I turn off the memories?"

"God can help you."

"I can't seem to get close to God. Maybe I never was."

"Never was what? Close to Him? Truly saved?"

"I thought I was, when I was ten years old. I believed everything the preacher said. Now, I'm beginning to doubt."

"Beginning to doubt? What?"

"Liz, I've been doing a lot of Bible stories for Christian magazines. I study them in depth and search my heart for the emotions, not just the actions, of all the ones involved in them. It seems like the more I get into them, the more incredible – and totally unrealistic - they become."

"So you're beginning to doubt the truth in the Bible?"

Dani swallowed and lowered her eyes. "Yes."

Silence prevailed.   What was Liz thinking, Dani wondered, that I'm the world's worst sinner and definitely on my way to hell?

"At some time or other, everyone has doubts," Liz finally said. "When that happens, we need to pray very hard for God to show us the truth. The Bible tells us we will know the truth and the truth will set us free."

Dani said nothing. For what seemed a very long time, there was silence between them, before Liz spoke again.

"Let's go for a walk. It's too pretty a day to just sit here."

"Are you sure you're up to it?"

Without answering, Liz started to stand but had a difficult time of it.

Laughing, Dani was to her feet quickly and giving her friend a hand. "Is it worth it?"

"All of it and more. Tom and I want this baby so much."

"James wants to start a family."

"That doesn't surprise me. He would make a wonderful father, just as Tom will. What do you think about it? Are you ready? You aren't getting any younger, you know."

"That's what he said, but he just refers to himself as getting older, never me."

"He's too polite to insinuate that you'll age, too, just like him."

They both laughed as they walked leisurely through the grass. At the edge of the yard, where the woods started, they stopped.

"I love this place," Liz said. "I mean, you have a lovely yard and neighbors but you also have this big, beautiful privacy barrier. Do you and James ever trek through the woods?"

"We used to, before we got too busy."

"Maybe that's the root of all your problems. You're too busy for each other. Maybe that's why Max looks so good and enticing, because you've stopped taking the time to see all that wonderful stuff in James. It's not that it isn't still there. It's just that you don't see it anymore."

"James still wants us to do things together. He's always talking about going on a vacation."

"Do it, Dani." Liz glanced at her watch. "I've got to go now."

They walked back to the house quietly, then down the driveway to Liz's car. After a brief hug, she was on her way home and Dani was once again alone.

Alone. Always alone.

SEVEN

SURPRISINGLY, THE AFTERNOON PASSED QUICKLY. Liz's visit had been uplifting, although equally disturbing. Dani decided not to dwell on the latter, but merely on how it always made her feel better to just be with her friend. There was something about her that was special. James said it was her genuine love and trust in God. Perhaps he was right.

How did one acquire that genuine love and trust? Dani looked up from her computer and stared ahead of her for several moments. It certainly wouldn't happen to someone who had doubts about the authenticity of the Bible.

Was that what happened to Eve? Had she simply just started doubting that God only wanted the best for her? Had she decided He kept the forbidden fruit from her and Adam because He didn't think they were worthy to eat it, and for no other reason?

Was Max her own personal forbidden fruit?

"I'm going to put him out of my mind. I'm going to forget about him and devote my every thought to my husband."

Her thoughts stopped abruptly. There it was again! That flash at the window. What in the world was going on? Not waiting for a chance to talk herself out of it, she ran to the door and flung it open. Someone was out there and she was going to find out who it was!

For several moments she looked all around her but saw nothing. Then she caught sight of something in the distance. "Wait! Who are you? Stop!" With a sudden, deep gasp, she didn't say another word. The image was suddenly clear enough to see and all she could do was look, unable to believe her eyes. What in the world? It couldn't be!

Running across the yard and then disappearing into the woods beyond it was......a nun!

"Oh, no, this is crazy!" She cried aloud as she stood perfectly still, staring until the figure was completely out of sight. "I'm seeing things. My eyes are playing tricks on me." She shook her head from side to side in disbelief.

She was so entranced that she never heard the vehicle pull into the driveway or the car door opening. She wasn't even aware someone had approached her until she heard a voice beside her.

She whirled around. "Max! What are you doing here?"

"You look like you just saw a ghost. Are you okay? I saw you standing here, staring and shaking your head and thought I'd better stop and see if you were okay. Are you? Are you all right?"

She swallowed. "I'm not sure. I think I'm seeing things." Not even the fact that Max was there, standing very close to her, swayed her thoughts.

"What kind of things?"

"You wouldn't believe it if I told you."

"Why don't you try me and see?"

At that very moment, it became apparent to her that she was standing on her front porch next to Max Baker and anyone who might be watching could easily see them. Hadn't she just finished telling herself she was going to forget him? She didn't need to have some gossip started. "You shouldn't be here. Why are you here?"

"I wasn't coming here. I'm on my way to work."

"Well, you'd better go then."

"Dani! What just happened?"

"Someone has been looking through the windows. It happened yesterday and again just now and when I came out to check, I saw who it was."

"So who was it? Should we call the police?"

"No."

"But if someone's been looking in the window....."

"It was a nun!"

His eyes widened, then he smiled and started to laugh. He couldn't help himself. "A nun?"

"Stop laughing. I saw her! I only saw her back but she was wearing a long black dress, with that black headpiece. Nobody dresses like that but the nuns."

Forcing sobriety, he said, "Okay, so it was a nun. Where did she go?"

"Into the woods."

"Into the woods?"

"She disappeared into the woods."

"Want to go look for her? I'll go with you, in case she's dangerous." He snickered.

"You don't believe me. It's true. I tell you, I saw her."

Without another word, he took her arm and pulled her with him across the yard. They walked quickly and were soon at the edge of the wooded area where she'd seen the person disappear. When she stopped, he nudged her on and they ran into the trees.

Several moments later, they stopped.

"Where could she have gone?" Dani asked.

"Maybe the Lord made her invisible so she could get away. I mean, a nun would be like an angel, wouldn't she?"

She met his eyes, hers flashing. "You still don't believe me. I'm going back to the house. I never should've come here with you anyway."

He didn't let go of her arm, but clutched it tighter instead. "But we are here. We're all alone. Nobody can see us. No neighbors that might gossip. Absolutely nobody."

God could. Where had that thought come from? Without taking time to ponder the question, she turned and started walking back.

He stopped her and pulled her into his arms.

Before she realized what was happening, he was pressing his lips against hers and kissing her deeply and passionately. She knew she should pull away. She knew she should put a stop to it immediately. But knowing what she should do and doing what her heart was screaming for her to do were not the same thing. She inched closer to him and hungrily returned the kiss.

"We're all alone, Dani," he whispered when he pulled his lips away. "I think we both want the same thing. Let's do it. Now."

Reality returned with a roaring thud. "No! Let me go!" Wriggling frantically, she managed to free herself. With angry eyes, she looked into his, only to see him laughing.

"At least I know where I stand now. The way you kissed me proves you want it just as much as I do. Think about it, honey. I'll be back." Turning, he walked away, leaving her staring after him.

Her heart was racing. What had she just done? She told herself it had only been a kiss. How long had it been since she'd kissed her husband the way she'd just kissed Max? Since she'd wanted her husband as much as she had wanted Max?

"Oh, God, help me!" she cried softly.

"God doesn't hear the prayers of people like you."

She whirled around, her eyes wide. Where had the soft female voice come from? Someone was there. Someone had seen her and Max together. "Who are you? Where are you?"

No one answered and there wasn't another sound. Had it only been her imagination? Was the guilt surging through her entire body strong enough to make her hear a voice that wasn't really there?

The nun! It had to be her. A religious person would say something like that, would tell her God wouldn't hear her prayer because of what she'd just done. "Where are you?" she called again.

There was still no answer. Finally, Dani started walking and was soon out of the woods and at the edge of her yard. The first thing she noticed was that Max's truck was gone but she wasn't at all consoled by the realization. He would be back, and he would be more demanding than ever. Bits and pieces of their time together eleven years ago ran through her mind. He'd always been aggressive, always wanting more than she was willing to give. She had finally decided it was the real reason he left her, because she wouldn't do what he wanted.

"And all of a sudden I've decided I want him back?" She scolded herself harshly. "Was I crazy or what? I don't want anything to do with him!"

Why had she kissed him the way she had? If God could forgive her for anything, she hoped it would be for that, and that James would never find out it had ever happened.

Because she loved her husband with all her heart. That stolen moment in the arms of another man had proven it to her beyond the shadow of a doubt.

EIGHT

SHE WAS STILL VISIBLY SHAKEN when James came in that evening. For the first time in a long time, she met him at the door and threw herself into his arms.

Surprised but pleased, he pulled her close as he kicked the door shut behind them. "Is something wrong?"

"I don't want you to go."

He pulled back, looking at her with wide, quizzical eyes. "You don't want me to go?"

"I don't want to be alone."

"Has something happened? Let's go sit down and talk." Never removing his arm from around her, he led her to the sofa and they sat down very close together. "You're trembling."

"Something did happen today. James, yesterday and today I thought I saw something at the window. Today, I ran outside – and I saw someone running into the woods."

He gasped. "Why didn't you call me?"

"I – was to shaken to know what to do. Besides, it was broad daylight." And Max was there.

"What difference does that make? People can harm you no matter what time of day it is. Did you see who it was?"

"Yes."

His eyes widened. "You know who it was?"

"No."

"But you just said……"

"It was a nun."

Deathly silence.

"Did you hear me? It was a nun."

"I thought that's what you said, but I'm having trouble believing you really did say that. You saw - a – nun looking in the window?"

"No, I didn't see her looking in the window. I saw her running into the woods. I saw her back. The long black dress, the black head piece."

He didn't speak.

She pulled away slightly. "You don't believe me."

"I don't know why you'd lie about it, but you have to admit, it is hard to believe. I mean, a nun? Running into the woods?"

"She had to be the one at the window. Maybe she stole the coffee and the milk."

He couldn't help it. He started to laugh.

"James!"

"I'm sorry, honey. I can't help it." He kept laughing, even though she stared at him with eyes filled with daggers as he did.

Finally, he managed to compose himself. "I really am sorry. Look, why don't you come with me to Atlanta? I'll be in meetings all day but you can go shopping. Then we'll go out for a good dinner and….."

"No, I can't. I didn't finish my story today and I have to turn it in first thing in the morning. I wish I could go, but I can't." For the first time in a long time, she meant what she was saying. She truly wanted to go with her husband. Suddenly, she wanted that more than she ever had.

"Won't you give up this freelancing? Or at least cut back? We don't get to do anything together."

She smiled. "I'm going to cut back. I promise. But I do have to meet this deadline. You know how responsible I am. They're depending on me."

He ran his fingers through her hair. "So am I." Standing up, he pulled her to her feet with him.

When he enclosed her in his arms, she felt the return of all the love she'd had for him. She welcomed the emotions surging through her and inched closer to him.

"I have a little time," he whispered.

She didn't answer. She simply walked with him across the floor toward their bedroom.

SHE WAS SLEEPING like a baby when something jolted her abruptly awake. Opening her eyes groggily, she sat up in bed, trying to see through the darkness. All the while, her heart was racing as the uppermost thought on her mind was that she was alone.

But she wasn't alone. Someone was in the house, in the kitchen. Trying to suppress her fear, she told herself if the nun had come back, surely she wouldn't hurt her. They were gentle souls, helpful to others, never harmful. Maybe she was hungry. Maybe she just needed some more coffee and milk. The thought brought a smile. If all the nun, or anyone else for that matter, wanted was a little food, she'd be all too happy to give it to them. They didn't have to steal it.

She glanced at the illuminated numbers on her bedside clock. Two a.m.! That brought on more fear. No one without harmful intent would be in another person's house, uninvited, at two o'clock in the morning.

If only she had a weapon. Many times James had tried to persuade her to let him buy a pistol but she always talked him out of it. She was terrified of guns and didn't want one in the house. She'd rather take her chances. Their home was secure, with locks and deadbolts, and they lived in a safe, close-knit community. She never felt threatened enough to think she'd ever need a gun for protection.

Until right now. Despite everything, someone had gotten into the house. Very quietly, she placed her feet onto the floor and into the pair of slippers she always kept nearby, then reached for her robe.

The sound came again. This time it was definitely the opening of the kitchen door. Was the intruder leaving? Should she just stay where she was until she was sure he was gone? Or was it a she? Was it the nun?

Standing very still, she waited, and couldn't suppress a sigh of relief when the door closed quietly. Just the same, she didn't move, but continued to stare into the darkness. What if he came back?

She swallowed and placed her hand over her pounding heart. Maybe she should stay locked in her room, call the police and wait for them to get there before she left it.

If only James was home!

After a long time of perfect quietness, she braved her way out of the bedroom, down the hallway and into the living room. The nearer she got to the kitchen, the faster and harder her heart thumped. Was she doing the right thing? What if the intruder hadn't left at all? What if he had just pretended to go? What if he knew she was on her way there and was waiting for her, quietly hidden in the corner?

She stopped and swallowed. Should she go on? Before she could give herself time to give in to her fear, she stepped boldly into the kitchen, placed her hand on the light switch and turned it on.

The room was empty. She was so relieved she nearly fell over, but instead she found herself whispering, "Thank you, Lord."

It had never occurred to her to ask for His help. That would have been the first thing James would have done. Liz, too.

Still trembling, she went to the sink and poured a glass of water, then began to sip it slowly. It was over. Maybe nothing had even happened. Maybe it had all been her imagination. Maybe no one had been there at all. Maybe she was still keyed up over the events of the day.

She started to smile, but it stopped on her lips when she noticed something on the table. It was a folded piece of paper. Going closer, she picked it up. Her eyes widened as she read the words, scrawled in small but dark letters.

"He owes me all. I owe him nothing. Keep this between us and all I'll ever do is take a few essentials that should be mine anyway. Tell the Starrman and I might tell him a thing or two about you and your boyfriend."

What in the world? She reread the words. 'He owes me all. I owe him nothing.' What did it mean? Who was the 'he' the writer was referring to? 'Tell the Starrman......' It was their last name. Whoever wrote this knew who they were. He also knew that James wasn't there, that she would find the note and not him. James was the 'he'.

'I might tell him a thing or two about you and your boyfriend.' He knew about her and Max. Her eyes widened. It wasn't any 'he' that wrote this.   It was the nun! There was no one else it could be. She'd seen them together. She was the voice she'd heard in the woods after Max left.

But why would a nun – a revered Catholic sister – be stealing, breaking into someone's home and resorting to blackmail? Was she pretending to be someone she wasn't?

What would she tell James? The truth, that Dani had sent Max away, or something lewd and vulgar that she had devised in her mind?

Would she be convincing enough to make James believe her?

The most puzzling question of all was one simple little word: WHY?

NINE

JAMES DIDN'T GET HOME until two days later. When he called to tell her he'd be gone that long, Dani decided it would be a good time to spend some time with her parents. Even though they lived only a few miles away, she seldom got to see them or spend time with them because – she stopped herself right there. There were any number of excuses she could come up with as to why she hardly ever saw her parents, but that's all they were. Excuses.

Gina and Mark Cabot were overjoyed when she arrived.

"I *will* have to work some while I'm here," she told her mother, "but not all the time."

The tall, slim lady kept smiling as she and her shorter, heavy-set husband walked their daughter into the house.

"I'll put your bag in your old room," her father said then, twitching his grey mustache as he spoke. "Be back in a few moments." He started up the stairs and was soon out of sight.

Gina turned to Dani and her eyes became quizzical. "So, Danita, what made you decide to come here right now? James is always having to go out of town but you never left home because of it. Are the two of you having problems?"

Dani couldn't help but remember their romantic evening together before James left. "Everything's fine with us, Mom. I just felt like getting away." She wanted to explain why she was suddenly frightened to be alone, but every time she thought of it, she recalled the words on the note she'd found. Perhaps it would be better not to tell anybody, not just James, about it. She couldn't help thinking of the irony of the situation. Just a few days ago, she wasn't sure if she even loved her husband any longer and now she was terrified of losing him.

If only she could talk to the person who had decided to blackmail her. If only she could find out why she was doing it. Dani was sure it was the nun. All evidence pointed to her, but she still found it hard to believe.

"Did you hear me, Danita?"

Dani turned to her mother. She'd been lost in her thoughts and hadn't heard any of what Gina had just said. "I'm sorry." She smiled sheepishly. "My mind wandered."

"I should say it did. You were a million miles away. Want to talk about it?"

"No, I'm back now, so if you'll repeat what you were saying, I swear I will listen."

"I was saying that I've invited Rita and Roy Baker over for dinner this evening. Honey, it's been set up for a while, before I knew you were coming. Rita and I have gotten really close lately and…."

Despite her promise to listen, Dani was taken aback by her mother's words. Rita and Roy Baker were Max's parents. She hadn't seen them since she and Max broke up, but she was always certain they blamed her for their son's leaving home and moving so far away.

"I hope you don't mind, dear," Gina continued. "I know you used to be very close to Max's parents, but I don't suppose you've seen them for a while."

Not for eleven years.

"I'm sure they'll be very happy to see you again. Rita mentions you often, asking how you are and everything."

Everything? What was everything?

Mark joined them again and Dani was glad for the reprieve.

"Why don't you and I go sit on the porch and talk a while?" Mark asked his daughter. "I know Gina wants to start on her dinner preparations and you know how your mother is, she doesn't want anyone else in the kitchen with her."

How well she remembered. Smiling, she followed her father outside and they sat down on the porch swing. They quickly fell into an easy conversation, just as they always managed to do, and she enjoyed being with him. Unlike her mother, he never said a word about the expected dinner guests.

When the doorbell rang sharply at six o'clock, Gina called to Dani from the kitchen, asking her to please let the Bakers in. She started toward the door, trying to prepare herself for what she would say to them. Had her mother told them she was there?

On the other side of the door stood Max. He was alone.

His eyes sparkled when he saw her. "Well, I never expected to be greeted by you, sweetheart. And to think, I tried every excuse I could come up with to get out of coming to this dinner. I'm glad none of them worked."

She turned away and started across the room.

He followed quickly and reached for her arm.

She pulled away immediately.

He whirled her around, forcing her to face him. "What's this all about? You act like you just let the devil in the door."

"Maybe I did."

He lowered his voice. "You sure weren't this cool with me the other day."

"Don't mention it again, Max. I'd like to pretend it didn't happen. It was a mistake."

"Well, it did happen and I don't consider it a mistake at all. I look at it more like a new beginning."

"I don't need a new beginning. I'm very happy with my husband and I'm very much in love with him."

He lowered his voice even more. "But it wasn't James you were kissing so passionately, was it?"

A sudden thought came to her. "Did you leave that note?"

His eyes narrowed quizzically. "Note?"

She sighed. "I don't know why I even asked."

"What kind of note are you talking about?"

"It's nothing."

"Does it have anything to do with that – person – we were chasing?"

She didn't answer.

He touched her arm but she quickly pulled away. "Look, Dani, maybe I did take advantage that day. So I'm a heel. You always knew that, but I do care what happens to you. If you're in some kind of trouble, let me help you."

Although she had no intention of telling him what had happened, she couldn't help being touched by his sudden tenderness. Long ago memories tried their best to surface, reminders of how he used to be. But that was a long time ago.

He placed his hands very gently beneath her chin and lifted her face. Their eyes met. "I'm sorry. I never meant to hurt you then – or now. Will you forgive me? Can we just start over as friends?"

They never heard anyone else until Max's father cleared his throat. Turning quickly, they saw both his parents watching them. His father was scowling. His mother had an unusual gleam in her eyes.

They must have left the door open. How else had they gotten in? How long had they been there? How much had they heard?

Dani forced a smile. "Rita! Roy! It's been such a long time!" Going to them, she hugged first one and then the other.

"It's so good to see you, Dani," Rita said. "It has been a long time."

"Is your husband here?" asked Roy, looking around as he spoke.

"No, he's out of town on business. I'm spending a few days with Mom and Dad while he's gone."

"I see," said Max's mother. As she spoke, she moved her eyes, first to Dani and then to her son. "How long have you been here, Max? You told me you weren't going to come."

Max grinned. "I changed my mind and I'm glad I did now. I mean, it's been forever since I've seen Dani. Marriage agrees with her, don't you think? Isn't she radiant? James is one lucky man."

The evening passed in a blur for Dani. As everyone sat around the table, talking and laughing, all she could think about was the passionate kiss she'd shared with Max. Was that the uppermost thought for him, too? In her heart, she regretted it and wished it had never happened. What might he be thinking, about when it would happen again?

Several times she looked up and found him staring at her. When he caught her eye, he simply grinned and turned away. Sometimes he would wink at her.

How many of those exchanges had the parents noticed?

When her cell phone rang and she saw James' number come up, she was never so happy to have an excuse to leave the room. Before long, she was lost in conversation with her husband and felt her tensions easing. But the call was over too quickly, and she felt a terrible loneliness within her heart. She wanted to with him. She wanted to go home. But James wasn't at home. He was still in Atlanta.

There was no one at home – unless the unknown, unwanted visitor decided to come back.

TEN

Dani ARRIVED HOME early Saturday morning. With dread in her heart, she started checking to see if anything was missing. There was plenty of coffee and milk and none of the goodies she always kept on the table had been touched. Nothing seemed to be missing from the pantry. All the canned goods were in order, the cereal boxes were full and all the pasta was there. Just as she started to breathe a sigh of relief, she opened the freezer. She gasped.   The steaks she had planned to fix for dinner were gone. Taking another look in the refrigerator, she discovered all the salad fixings were gone as well. A recheck of the pantry showed an empty spot where the potatoes should have been. Frantically, she checked all the other cabinets but didn't find anything else missing.

The visitor had come in and helped herself while she'd been gone. How many times had she been there in the last two days? How had she gotten in? If one person could get in so easily, could others do the same thing?

Since she was convinced the robber had definitely been the nun she'd seen running into the woods that day, she didn't feel threatened by her.   It still seemed ridiculous and impossible that someone in a religious position could be breaking into her home and taking things from it, but she wasn't fearful that she would physically harm her. What bothered her was what she might do verbally. She thought again of the note she had hidden in her bureau drawer. She'd read it over and over so many times she had it memorized. The more she thought of it, the more terrified she became that this person could do serious harm to her marriage.

She truly loved her husband. Any doubts she'd had when Max had so suddenly reappeared were gone. If only she hadn't given in to that one forbidden pleasure when she kissed him so passionately in the woods that day.

How many times did Eve regret her decision? Just one bite was all it took and she lost everything that was good and wonderful in her life. Would finding out about just that one kiss be enough to make James begin to doubt Dani, even if he believed her when she told him how she regretted it? Would he ever trust her again, fully and completely?

James didn't deserve such betrayal. He had never done a thing to hurt her or make her suspicious of his love. All he'd ever been was good, kind, loving and faithful.

A tear ran down her cheek. She would never tell him about the note. If he didn't read it, he wouldn't question it.

She forced herself to stop thinking. She had to get to the store and replace all the missing items, all the things she needed for the special dinner she'd promised James that evening. She'd buy some candles for the table. Maybe she'd get a sweet but sentimental card and put it somewhere he'd find it when he wasn't expecting it.   She smiled. She would get all dressed up and fix her hair the way he liked it. Later, after they were totally relaxed and contented.....her smile turned into a huge grin, then to laughter. Oh, she could hardly wait for that!

She was surprised when she met Liz at the checkout line. "You mean Tom still lets you do the shopping? That cart is full and it's going to be a lot for you to handle."

"Not since you're here! You can put everything in the car and Tom will take it out. See how the Lord works everything out."

"You're sure he'll be home when you get there?"

"Of course. He said he would and he'll be there. Is James back yet?"

"He should be home in a couple more hours."

They walked through the parking lot and stopped by Liz's car. "Do you know what?" Liz said then. "I am craving a McDonald's ice cream cone. It would only take a minute to run by and get one."

"I can't let these steaks stay in the car too long."

"But they're in the cold sack."

Dani laughed. "Yes, they are. Let's go."

She told Liz to go sit down and she would order. As she waited in line, she glanced around as she usually did. Everything was the same as it ever was, people standing around talking, kids begging to be allowed to go to the play room. Her eyes stopped on one lone figure in the corner. It was a young girl, probably about 18 or 19, with long straight dark hair. She was dressed in black from head to toe. Black jeans, black shirt and black boots. What caught Dani's attention was the seriousness of the girl's expression and the way she seemed to be staring at her. Or was she looking at someone else? Dani glanced around to see there was no one behind her in the line. Reverting her eyes to the young girl, Dani smiled at her, but the girl only continued to stare with what appeared to be a perpetual frown on her lips. Too bad she was so solemn, Dani thought. She would be very pretty otherwise.

It was her turn to order. When she turned around again, holding the two ice cream cones in her hands, the girl was gone.

She told Liz about it. "She was strange," she finally concluded. "It kind of gave me the willies, the way she was looking at me."

Liz licked her ice cream. "Oh, I'd forgotten how good this is! Is she still here, Dani? Maybe we should talk to her. Maybe she's in trouble and needs to talk to somebody."

Dani laughed. "That sounds just like you. I don't know where she went. She was there and when I turned around after I ordered, she was gone." Dani took a lick. "I wonder why she kept staring at me. I was kind of glad when she wasn't there anymore."

"Well," Liz replied, her eyes suddenly very serious, "if she comes back, we'll ask her if she wants a cone."

They laughed together and for a few minutes there was silence as they enjoyed their treat.

Then Liz said. "So how are your mom and dad?"

"Good."

"Why'd you go there?"

"It was time, don't you think?"

"You've never just taken off on the spur of the moment and gone someplace and stayed there two days, not even to your parents' house. Every time James goes out of town, you use every free moment to get caught up on your writing. Never once have you just taken off like this. Does it have anything to do with Max?"

"Why would you ask something like that?"

"For one thing, I wonder if he might be trying to come on to you and if he knows James is gone, he might take advantage. I know Max, remember? But then again, I know Max's parents live really close to your parents, and he might even be staying there with them. Maybe you're the one wanting to see him."

"That's not fair, Liz."

"Tell me then."

"I love James. Yes, I was surprised when I saw Max again and, yes, I was confused and emotional. But seeing him again did me a favor. It made me realize how very much I love my husband and how glad I am that I married the man I did."

Liz waited silently.

"That's all," Dani finally said.

Liz sighed and took another lick of her ice cream.

'She knows I'm leaving something out,' Dani thought. 'But I can't tell her. I can't tell anyone the real reason I left. No one must ever find out about that threatening note, and how it made me afraid to stay home alone. No one. Not even my best friend.'

ELEVEN

For the next several days, James was preoccupied with the plans for the complex computer system he would soon be installing. He worked late every day and was so dead tired and emotionally drained when he got home that he fell into bed almost as soon as he got there.

Dani kept writing, deciding to wait until he had a chance to slow down before she cut back on her own assignments. She had just been given a new one, but she was having a difficult time getting into it. Every time she started to try to write, her mind would start wandering, and it was usually back to the story of Adam and Eve. Why was it so intriguing to her? She longed to know more, to know all the details of the lives of the first man and woman, but the Bible was pretty vague about it. Why didn't it tell more?

What were they really like? As husband and wife, were they totally satisfied with each other, or did they wonder if there might be something else out there that would make them happier? Did they love each other deeply, or did they merely tolerate one another because they had no other choice? How many of their traits had she inherited?

With a deep sigh, she stood up from her computer and stretched. "If I had one wish," she said aloud, "I would wish to go back in time and actually become Eve. I guess that's the only way I'd ever know how she truly felt." She laughed softly at the thought and went to the kitchen for some coffee.

It was so quiet around. If only James would come home early. There was no chance of that, but at least she knew he would be home before dark. Soon, he would be going back to Atlanta and she dreaded the thought of it. Should she go with him? There was no telling how long he would have to stay and she had no idea what she'd do while he was working. She shrugged her shoulders. The same thing she'd be doing at home, working on her own assignments. She could do some shopping, but shopping alone in a place where she didn't know anyone would quickly become tiresome and boring. Besides, there was nothing she needed to buy.

Picking up the phone, she dialed her husband's number. "Is there any way we could meet somewhere for lunch, or even just a cup of coffee?" she asked as soon as he answered.

She could hear his smile as he replied. "Honey, I'd like nothing better."

Seated across the table from one another in their favorite restaurant a short time later, they talked softly. They discussed the weather, the current events and other trivial things before he asked her if she'd had any more time to consider going on a vacation.

Her eyes lit up. "Oh, let's do it, James! I want to."

He laughed. "Well, this is a surprise, but a good one. Where shall we go and when? It can be any time after I finish up this Atlanta job – a couple weeks at the most."

"I'll be thinking on it and we'll make up our minds."

"I can't help wondering what's happened to you in the last few days, Dani. You've changed. Don't misunderstand me. I love the change. You're more like the young bride I had ten years ago than the bored, married woman you seemed to becoming. To be honest, I was getting worried about our relationship, but after the last week," he winked and grinned, "well, I'm convinced you do still love me."

She smiled. "I do love you, James."

"I'd like to ask you something."

She waited.

"Tom says you and that young man we met at dinner last week, Max Baker, used to be a little more than friends."

Taken by surprise, she looked away from him. As she did, she caught sight of the same young girl she'd seen in McDonald's Saturday evening. She didn't know what made her heart start racing faster, James' question or seeing the girl. She was dressed the same way, all in black, and she was staring at her just as intently as she'd done the other time.

"Dani?"

She turned back to James. "I didn't know Tom knew that. Liz must have told him." What all had her best friend revealed to her husband? Had she mentioned how emotionally shaken Dani had been or told him any of the things Dani had said to her in confidence?

Her eyes wandered back to the corner. The girl was still there, still staring, still wearing her perpetual frown.

"She mentioned it after they went home that night, but he said she didn't say anything else other than the fact the two of you used to be a really hot item."

A really hot item. "We were teen agers. I was 17 and he was 18. We thought we were in love."

"What happened?"

"James, I've never quizzed you about any of your old sweethearts. What does it matter what happened? It's over and done."

"Mary Narby met me a couple days ago when I went outside to get the mail. She told me she'd seen a handsome young man standing on the porch talking to you about a week ago. She described Max."

Mary Narby. Their neighbor. "Why didn't you ask me about it before?"

"I guess I was hoping you'd just tell me. She says the two of you ran off toward the woods and then disappeared for a little while."

If only her heart would slow down! "We did. That was the day I saw the nun. I was standing on the porch, watching her, and Max just happened to be driving by on his way to work. He stopped to see if I was all right. We ran into the woods together to see if we could find her, but we couldn't."

James smiled. "I figured as much. I never have worried about gossip from busy-body neighbors. I just wanted to hear what you had to say about it." He reached over and squeezed her hand. "I trust you, Dani."

Oh, James! She smiled back at him.

"I've gotta run now, honey. I should be able to get home early today. We'll go get some pizza and go to a movie, if there's anything good playing. If you want to."

"That sounds like fun. I'm going to stay a little while and have another cup of coffee. See you later."

"I love you." He stood up, bent down and kissed her lips gently and then left.

Watching him leave, she had a mixture of feelings. She'd told him only half the truth. What would he think of her if he knew what had happened while she and Max were in the woods that day? Would he still be wanting to take her out that evening, or would he be wanting to pack his bags and leave her?

She looked again to the corner. The girl was still there.

'I'm going over to her,' she thought, 'and ask her why she keeps staring at me like that. She looks like she's mad at me about something, almost like she hates me and I have no idea why. But I'm going to find out – right now!'

Before she could stand up, she caught sight of none other than Max, walking toward her and smiling. There was no way she could avoid him without causing a scene. All she could do was sit there and wait.

Without being invited, he sat down across from her in the chair James had just left. "I didn't expect to see you, Dani. Fate just seems to be throwing us together."

She didn't look at him. As if on their own accord, her eyes reverted back to the corner. The girl was still there, still watching.

Max waved his hand in front of her face, catching her attention. "You okay?"

"I'm fine. I was just leaving, so if you'll excuse me." She started to stand up.

"Whoa!" Placing his hand on her arm, he nudged her back down. "I didn't come over here to bite you or eat you up, sweetheart. I just happened to see you and wanted to say hello, like any good friend would do.”

Her eyes met his. “You aren’t just any good friend.”

He grinned. “I like the sound of that. I was hoping I was more than that to you.”

“That’s not what I meant and you know it.”

“What I know is that I want you back, and after that kiss, well, I’m not thoroughly convinced you don’t want me, too.”

“Max, don’t talk so loud. Somebody might hear you.”

He laughed. “Sorry. We wouldn’t want our little secret to come out, would we?   Not yet anyway.”   Totally unexpectedly, he leaned over and kissed her cheek.

She jumped to her feet before he could stop her again. “Not yet. Not ever,” she seethed.

He stood up, too, and without a word walked toward the door beside her. Just as she started to open it, it opened from the other side and there stood James.

Her eyes widened. “James, I thought you were gone.”

He looked at her, then at Max, then back to her. “I left my cell phone on the table. Did you see it? Do you have it?”

“I’m sorry, I didn’t see it there.”

“Perhaps you were too distracted.” Without another word, he walked away, headed back to the table they’d just left.

Dani turned to Max, daggers in her eyes. “Stay away from me, Max Baker.”

He simply chuckled, opened the door and went outside.

Dani waited for James to return. After a seemingly long time, he finally got back to her. “Did you find it?”

"It was on the floor. I must have dropped it." He met her eyes. "Is there some reason he was here with you just now?"

Was he angry? She'd never seen James angry, but she'd never seen him so seriously solemn either. "No," she said softly. "He was just here and saw me."

"Just like the day on the porch?"

"Yes."

"You were distracted before I left. Is it because of him? Did you see him then?"

"No. I saw someone else."

They walked outside together. "Someone else?"

"It's a girl. She's all dressed in black and….."

"The same one you told me was in McDonald's?"

"Yes. She's always staring at me. Every time I look at her, she's staring at me. I don't know if she was here by coincidence or if – or if – she's stalking me."

To her surprise, her husband snickered. "Was she really here or is she a convenient excuse?"

His words stung. "I'm telling the truth."

"We'll talk later. I have to go."

No hug. No kiss. No I love you. He just simply walked away.

TWELVE

"I'M SORRY, DANI. I shouldn't have jumped to conclusions, but when I saw him standing there with you, it just flew all over me. I wanted to literally knock his lights out. I want you to know that I believe you, that he just happened to be there, that it was an accidental meeting. Can you forgive me?"

Lying in bed next to her husband, listening to his even breathing as he slept, Dani heard his words again in her mind. He wanted her to forgive him. She should be asking him to forgive her. She should tell him the truth about that day in the woods. Everything about it. How she wanted to kiss Max as much as he wanted to kiss her. How she urged him on. And how she regretted it. How it had actually opened her eyes to the extreme depth of her love for her husband. That she knew for a certainty she had never loved Max the way she loved him.

Would he still insist that he believed her about all of it, or would he only believe the part about the intimate kiss?

"I was such a fool," she told herself. "I was just like Eve, craving the one thing that was forbidden over the beauty of what I already had." With a sigh, she quietly slipped out of the bed, put on her robe and slippers and left the room. It was apparent she wasn't going to sleep, so she may as well work a while.

The story wasn't going well at all. As she sat at her computer, trying to put real, true emotions into the lives of characters in the Bible who had lived thousands of years ago, trying to make them believable and real, she found herself staring at a nearly empty screen. It hadn't been this difficult with Adam and Eve.   As she'd done countless times before, she asked herself if it was so easy to write about Eve because she was so much like her.

Her thoughts were swayed when she had a sudden feeling of being watched. She looked all around, seeing nothing but the emptiness of the room and hearing nothing other than her own breathing in the quietness. For a while, she sat perfectly still, waiting. For what, she had no idea. Just waiting.

The sensation remained, making her more and more uneasy. What was it? She'd worked countless times in the wee hours of the night and never been spooked before.

But that was before somebody started coming into her home and stealing things. She knew it was the nun she'd seen running that day. What if it wasn't the nun this time? What if someone else was actually standing outside her window, watching every move she made?   What if someone was waiting for a chance to get in, to slip up on her? What if someone was already in the room, hiding in the corner?

She swallowed, trying to rid herself of the panic she felt swelling in her throat. She told herself all she had to do was get up, leave the room and go back to the bedroom. James was there. He wouldn't let anyone harm her.

She couldn't move. What if someone jumped on her the minute she tried to stand up? James! Her mind cried out for her husband but no sound would come from her lips.

There was a scratching sound at the window and she jumped. Someone was there, but he was outside, not in. Her survival instincts kicked in and she leapt to her feet. In an instant, she'd turned off the light and ran to the window, pulling back the heavy drapery. In the light of the moon, she saw nothing. Absolutely nothing.

"Dani?"

The light came on again and she ran to James, throwing herself into his arms.

"Dani, what's wrong? I woke up and discovered you weren't in bed and when I came in here, it was all dark. Are you okay?"

She was shivering so much she couldn't speak.

He held her tightly for a moment, then released his grip, gently pushing her back to look at her.

"I felt like somebody was watching me. I thought he was outside, but then I thought he might be in the room and then I heard something at the window — but nothing was there!"

"You stay here and I'll look around, okay?"

"There's no one here. I think it was all in my imagination. Ever since somebody broke in and took the coffee and milk, I've been squeamish."

For a moment his eyes were quizzical. Then realization dawned. "I'd just about forgotten the coffee and milk incident."

"It was the nun that took them. I'm sure of it, and I'm not afraid of her. I mean, a nun wouldn't hurt me."

"I don't think a nun would steal coffee and milk either."

He had no way of knowing about the other missing food items — the steak, salad fixings and potatoes. Or the note.

"Dani?"

"I don't know what got into me." Forcing a smile, she backed away from him slightly. "Maybe I shouldn't have gone to that scary movie tonight."

"It was pretty bad, wasn't it? Now, why don't we go into the kitchen and have a glass of milk and....oh, I forgot you don't like milk. Let's just have a glass of water. Maybe a cookie."

She smiled. "Then I'll get a sugar high and won't be able to sleep."

"Apparently, you couldn't sleep anyway or you wouldn't have gotten up and gone to your office." Placing his arm around her again, he led her from the room.

The cookie canister was empty.

Their eyes met.

"I just filled it up yesterday," she said softly, a slight tremor in her voice.

He didn't say anything for a moment.

"She must have come back," Dani went on.

"You're so certain this nun you think you saw is the one stealing our groceries, aren't you?"

"I don't think I saw her. I did! She ran into the woods."

"But there was no sight of her when you followed her. You and Max Baker." He emphasized Max's name.

"No. She got away."

"Well, I think it's time to have a little talk with the sheriff. No matter who you think is doing it, someone is breaking into our home and stealing things. And I have no idea how he is getting in. There's never been any sign of a forced entry. And why is nothing except food ever seem to be missing?"

"Maybe she's hungry."

"And maybe it's not a 'she' but a 'he'. Or a 'they'."

"I don't think we should involve the police. Not yet." What if they somehow forced her to tell them about the note?

"This is an exasperating situation and you are exasperating, my lovely wife. Think about it this way. We need to get this checked out because I'm not always going to be here with you if something more happens."

"What do you mean?"

"As frightened as you were right now, what are you going to do when I go back to Atlanta next week?"

"Next week? You're going next week?"

"I have to. We've got to get this job done."

"I was thinking of going with you." She met his eyes anxiously.

"You can go if you want, but I'll forewarn you. I'll probably be on the job from sun up to sun down, for as long as it takes to finish, which could be a week or more. There's a lot of teeny weeny details and every one of them has to be worked out perfectly. I'm afraid you'd be bored to death."

"I could do my writing there, just like I do here."

He kissed the top of her head. "Let's go back to bed. We can talk about it some more in the morning."

She took his hand and they started walking across the room.

"I don't ever want to think you're in danger when you're here alone, Dani, and I don't want you to think that way either. Whether or not we go to Atlanta together, we still have to find out exactly who has been getting into our home. I don't want you here alone, unprotected, and I don't want our home unprotected when neither one of us is here. Do you understand what I'm saying?"

"We could buy a security system. We talked about it lots of times."

"We will, but we'll also report this to the sheriff. If someone's getting into our home, he may be getting into others' homes, too."

"They'll laugh when we tell them the thief only takes food."

"Do we know that's true? There might be other things that we just haven't missed yet."

"I'm sure there isn't. Someone is just hungry. I mean, why else would they want milk and cereal, coffee, steak and...." She stopped, realizing what she'd just said.

"Steak?"

She sighed. "I guess I forgot to tell you about that. It happened when I was at Mom and Dad's house."

He stopped and looked deeply into her eyes. "Anything else you forgot to tell me?"

Only about a note that could ruin our marriage. "No."

THIRTEEN

BEFORE IT WAS TIME FOR JAMES TO LEAVE AGAIN, Dani came up with the perfect solution. She would spend the nights with Liz while he was gone. That way, she could be at home during the day and keep up with her writing as well as everything else she needed to do. As long as it was daylight outside, she would have no reason not to feel safe. Before James had to go anyplace else, they would have time to get the security system they ordered in place.

Sunday morning, the day before he had to leave, James was up earlier than usual and when Dani went into the kitchen she found him dressed in his best suit and tie.

After a quick thought as to her own attire, her old robe and slippers and tousled hair, she smiled. "Boy, do you look nice! What are you all dressed up for?" Going over to him, she crawled onto his lap, snuggled against him and kissed him lightly. "Umm. You smell good, too."

He looked deeply into her eyes. "I'm doing something I've been putting off way too long. I'm going to church. I'm hoping you'll go with me."

"Do I have time to get ready?"

"We don't have to leave for a couple hours."

"I guess I'll go. It's something different to do."

His eyes turned very serious. "Oh, Dani, we don't go to church just to have something different to do. We go because we love the Lord and want to worship Him with other believers. I've really been feeling guilty lately about staying away so long and I want to start going regularly."

"But you're so busy. You put in so many hours at work during the week. Sunday's the only day you have to relax, the only day we have together. That is, when you aren't working then, too."

"I'm going to hire some more helpers so I can cut down on my working schedule. We need more time together and we need to make time to go to church on Sunday."

"You're really serious."

"I am."

"Has something happened?"

"Why do you ask that?"

"People usually start getting serious about religion when they're in trouble or when they're sick. You aren't sick, are you?"

He grinned. "I'm not sick and I'm not in trouble, and I'm not talking about religion. I'm talking about being a true Christian. Look at it this way. If I should get sick or get into trouble, I want my heart to be in good standing with God when it happens. If I keep ignoring Him, He'd have every right to ignore me if I really needed Him."

"Do you think He won't hear your prayers if you don't start going to church? Is that it?"

"He will always hear my prayers and He will always answer in the way that's best, whether or not I am a faithful church-goer. I believe that. But it makes me feel guilty to always be expecting Him to do things for me, while I never do anything for Him."

"But you pray all the time. That's proof that you believe in Him. That's doing something."

"It's important to go to church, too. It helps us grow in our spiritual life, and when we grow, we can help others who are lost to find the right path in life."

She nuzzled against him. "You sound so serious."

"I am serious, honey. I told you that already. I'm serious about doing more for the Lord, learning more about Him, and doing more for others through His love."

She kissed his cheek and stood up. "I'll go get ready."

She was sure she enjoyed the service as much as he did, even though she felt a few sharp pricks inside her heart several times. Especially when the minister's entire sermon was based on the truth and authenticity of The Holy Bible.

The rest of the day passed much too quickly. Never before did she dread so much for her husband to leave her. It wasn't because she didn't want to be alone or because she was frightened. It was simply because she could hardly stand the thought of him not being there.

He detained his trip by a couple hours when they got up Monday morning to find several food items missing from the pantry. Despite his wife's pleas not to involve the police, he went to the sheriff and filed a report. Even though they promised to have a patrol car drive by their home as often as they could, he insisted Dani stay at Liz's the entire time he was gone and not just at night. Reluctantly, she agreed.

He never left the house until she had packed her bag and was on her way to her friend's place.

It didn't take long for Dani to get homesick. Although she and Liz enjoyed being together, she missed being home. She didn't feel like there was any danger there as long as it was still daylight. A little over a week later, against the protests of her friend and without telling James, she headed back to their house. Even if she didn't stay, she needed to check on things.

She was particularly happy that day. The sun was big and beautiful amid the bright blue sky and the silhouette of the mountains in the background was breathtaking. She loved living in western North Carolina. No matter how many places she'd been, she couldn't envision any of them being lovelier.

She was relieved when nothing else seemed to be missing from the kitchen. The visitor, as she started referring to the nun she was sure was responsible for the thefts, apparently wasn't interested in anything else in the house. Only food. Her heart lurched at the thought of anyone being so hungry she resorted to stealing to fill her stomach. She would willingly give food away to anyone who needed it.

Could the nun be living nearby? How was she able to get back and forth so quickly and often? There was no convent in the area. Perhaps she'd left the religious order and was in hiding somewhere. Where could she be? Dani knew there were several trailers not far from where the woods stopped and that poorer people lived there. It would be possible to get there by taking a shortcut through the woods. She wasn't about to go into them alone but maybe she could take a drive around them and through the area, just to take a look around. Anyone wearing a long dress and veil couldn't be hard to spot unless she was intentionally hiding herself.

What would she do if she saw her? She decided she'd figure that out if and when it happened.

The more she thought of it, the more the idea intrigued her. Before she could talk herself out of it, she was in her car and headed for the trailer park.

She drove through slowly, her eyes scanning everything in sight. It saddened her to see such poverty. Even though she'd known about it, she'd never actually been in the midst of it. She wondered if there was anything she could do to help some of these people. There were little children running around playing, dressed in nothing more than rags. Dirty ones at that. Older folks stood around talking, smoking cigarettes and holding beer cans. She sighed. If they could afford cigarettes and beer, couldn't they afford to put better clothing on their children? And couldn't they afford food?

After she'd driven through the very last road in the court, she turned around. There was nothing here to help her solve the mystery of the robberies taking place in her home. With a sigh, she stopped at the end of the development, ready to pull back onto the highway.

A tapping on her car window caught her attention and she turned to see who it was. She couldn't believe her eyes when she saw none other than the young girl dressed in black that she'd seen twice in the last few days. She quickly rolled down her window.

The girl scowled at her. "What are you doing here?"

Dani smiled, thinking again how pretty she would be if only she would smile in return. Seeing her up close, she noticed that her eyes were much darker than she thought. Her skin was clear and flawless, and her long, straight black hair was shiny and silky. One word came to mind to describe her. She was beautiful.

"I was just driving through," Dani said, hoping she could strike up a conversation and learn more about this mysterious stranger. "Do you live here?"

"I wouldn't be here if I didn't, would I? I certainly wouldn't be driving here at all if I had a car like this. What did you come for, to look down on us?"

"No. I don't look down on you at all. I was – just out for a drive and....."

"And you just happened to see this run down trailer court and wanted to take a closer look at it. Come on now!"

Dani's heart started racing. This girl was filled with anger and she had no idea what to say to help her. "What's your name?"

The girl smirked. "What's it matter to you?"

"Maybe I'd like to say a prayer for you." Dani's words surprised herself probably more than the young girl. She hadn't planned to say them. They just came out of her mouth.

The girl laughed, but sobered again quickly. "You may as well save your breath, lady. God doesn't recognize my name. He never has and never will."

What could she say to that? Could she convince her that God loved her, even as she sat there in her expensive car, as the girl had just pointed out, looking at the rundown place where she lived? "I have an idea," she said then, even as she wondered what it was.

"So I've had lots of ideas but they never did me any good."

"I was thinking maybe we could go get a little something to eat. It's already lunch time and I'm hungry and I hate to eat by myself. We could talk a bit, maybe get acquainted."

"You know, you crack me up. I don't need a good Samaritan in my life."

After a moment of silence, Dani said, "I've seen you a couple times lately. Every time I looked at you, you were staring at me and I'm wondering why."

The girl laughed. "One of these days, you'll know why and then you'll wish you didn't." Without another word, she turned and walked away quickly, leaving Dani astounded and speechless.

FOURTEEN

SHE SIGHED AS SHE HUNG UP THE PHONE after talking to James. She hadn't expected him to be happy about her going back home or about her drive through the trailer park, but she didn't think he'd actually yell at her. James never raised his voice and she didn't speak for several moments, waiting for him to calm down. He did, of course, and apologized, telling her she was going to worry him to death if she didn't promise to stay with Liz and not do any more dangerous snooping.

Dangerous snooping? All she'd done was take a drive.

When the phone rang again, almost immediately, she answered quickly. Knowing her husband, he was calling back to apologize again.

It wasn't James. It was her mother. They chatted for a while, about all the trivial things they always talked about, before Gina Cabot's voice softened and she told her daughter that Rita Baker, Max's mother, was quite possibly dying.

Dani's eyes widened. "Dying? She seemed fine when I saw her last week. What happened, Mom? Has she been in an accident or something?"

"No, nothing like that. She's had cancer for over a year now and the treatments aren't working for her."

"I'm really sorry to hear that. Why didn't you say something to me while I was there?"

"You were distracted, dear. You had no idea I knew how far away your mind was, but I did, even though you never said anything. I'm still wondering why, all of a sudden, you decided to come and spend two full days, but I'll not ask. If you want me to know, you'll tell me."

It was on the tip of Dani's tongue to tell her about the visitor coming to the house and stealing food and how she didn't want to stay there alone while James was away. She decided not to. Why worry Gina with such a petty little thing? They'd enjoyed their time together and it saddened Dani that she hadn't spent more time with her parents, for no other reason than wanting to be with them. "Mom, is Rita really dying? Is there nothing more that can be done for her if the treatments aren't working?"

"They've tried various things, but the doctors have given up hope. It breaks my heart. I told you that we've gotten very close lately. Even when you and Max were dating, we barely knew each other but then a couple years ago, we ran into each other while we were shopping and one thing led to another. We started visiting and going to dinner together. Your father and Roy aren't as close as Rita and I, but for my sake, he tolerates him." Gina chuckled. "You know your father. He has a hard time looking at Roy and not remembering how his son broke your heart all those years ago."

Dani had no idea her breakup with Max had weighed so heavily on her father's heart. But then again, she was living at home at the time and he couldn't help but see her crying every day from morning to night.

"Now, Rita and I," Gina continued, "have been able to get over it. After all, it isn't the parents' fault when their child does something they don't approve of."

"I always felt like she blamed me for everything."

"Why would you feel that way?"

"For one thing, we used to be pretty close, but after the break up, she more or less just started snubbing me and finally cut me entirely out of her life."

"You were so devastated, dear. I believe it was mostly your imagination, but well, it's all water under the bridge now, isn't it? Now, since she's so sick, it would be nice if you would call her once in a while, maybe even visit her. She mentions you often and I believe it would make her happy."

"I don't know, Mom. I think it's better to leave things as they are, especially since Max is back living with them again. It wouldn't look good for me to start coming around, with him there."

"But you could call her."

Dani said nothing.

"You need to make it soon, honey. I don't think she has much time left."

"You really think it's that bad?"

"I do, dear."

Dani sat with the phone dangling in her fingers after the conversation with her mother ended. It saddened her to hear of Rita's illness, but after all these years, wouldn't it make her wonder why she was doing it if she suddenly started calling her? She thought of the way Rita and Roy had walked into the house that evening and seen her and Max standing so close to each other, with his hands beneath her chin and their eyes locked. If, just out of the blue, Dani started calling her, would she start wondering if she was still in love with Max, despite the fact she was married? Would she think she was trying to get him back by getting back into the good graces of his parents?

And what about Max?

She thought of the times she'd seen him lately. How many times had it been, four, five, more?   First, it was in the parking lot. He had been friendly and they'd talked like two old friends, instead of two former lovers, until he'd commented how he regretted leaving her. Then, he'd coerced her into dancing with him when she was out with her husband and friends. There had been nothing secretive in his intentions then. Nor the day he kissed her. She flinched, remembering. She didn't want to think about that kiss and how shamelessly she had returned it, urging it to continue. Forcing her mind to go on, she thought of the next time they'd met, in the restaurant. How conveniently he had appeared almost the moment her husband had left. Then, he was at her parents' house the very evening she arrived. Had he known she would be there?

Was he watching her? Stalking her? Her eyes widened. If he was, she wasn't going to help him along by trying to form a new relationship with his mother after all these years. Gina might be exaggerating about Rita's state of health. Her mother was known to do that.

She finally convinced herself that was the case. She wasn't going to worry about it and she wasn't going to call Rita Baker. It would be best to let everything stay just as it was, as it had been for the last eleven years.

She was surprised when she looked up suddenly and discovered how dark the room had become. She didn't think she'd been on the phone that long. Looking at the time, she saw it was only a little after three. It must be clouding up. She went to the window and looked outside to see thick, dark clouds covering the sky. It was coming a storm and she needed to get back to Liz's place before her friend decided to send a police escort for her. She grinned at the thought, but she could still imagine it actually happening. As she locked up the house and started to her car, she sighed inwardly. She hadn't gotten one single word written on her last story. She wasn't going to have to worry about lessening her workload. She was going to wind up being fired!

FIFTEEN

SHE REACHED LIZ'S HOUSE just as the downpour started. As she ran from the car to the door, the lightning flashed wickedly all around her and the thunder roared angrily. She was never so glad to get inside and leave it on the outside behind her.

Why was it so dark? Was the power out? She flipped the light switch and light flooded the room, making her more curious than ever. Why were the lights out? "Liz!" Maybe she was lying down. She was very tired lately and needed a lot of rest. Dani rapped on the door. "Liz?" Opening it slightly, she saw the bed was empty. Going from room to room, she discovered that Liz wasn't in any of them.

Where could she be? She'd gotten groceries just the other day, so she wouldn't be at the grocery store. Liz rarely went anyplace else by herself because of her advanced pregnancy, and Tom would be at work so he wouldn't be with her.

If something came up and she had to leave, why hadn't she called to tell her? She would have returned immediately and taken her wherever she needed to go. She looked outside. Sure enough, Liz's car was gone. She hadn't even noticed when she'd drove in.

The baby! Had she gone into early labor and had to go to the hospital? Dani's eyes widened as she hurriedly pulled out her phone and dialed Liz's cell phone.

The phone rang and rang and then went to Voice Mail.

Immediately, she dialed Tom.

"Tom Grant. How can I help you?"

"It's Dani, Tom. Do you know where Liz is?"

"Dani? Where are you? Liz is at home."

"No, she's not. I'm at your house and she's not here."

"Not there? When did she leave?"

"I don't know. I was gone for a while and I just got back and she's not here."

"She didn't call and tell me she was going anyplace. Let me try her cell."

"I just did. It went right to Voice Mail! Tom, her car's gone. I'm frightened."

"Sit tight, Dani. I'll make some calls. I'll get back with you."

She could hear the fear in his voice before he hung up. Who was he going to call? Where was Liz?

She called James.

"She probably just went to the store. Maybe she's out of the service area, the reason you can't get her on her phone."

"There's service almost everywhere now. James, I'm scared! What if something happened to her? What if she's had an accident or something? You need to say a prayer. NOW."

He did just that. "Now, you say one, too."

"Out loud?"

"It doesn't matter. If it makes you uncomfortable to say it aloud, say it silently. God hears you either way."

She started to cry. "Oh, if anything's happened to her, I'll never forgive myself. I should've been here with her. I never should've gone to the house. I shouldn't have wasted time at that trailer park. I should have come back before I stayed on the phone so long with Mom. I……"

"Dani! Stop! None of this is your fault. If Liz went someplace, she went because she wanted to."

"Oh! A call's coming in. It's Tom. I'll call you back." She answered the other call. "Tom? Have you found her?"

His voice broke when he spoke. "No. I've called the sheriff and he's sending someone out to look." Lightning flashed, causing the phone line to crackle. "I'm going out, too, right now. I'll let you know as soon as I have any news."

She called James back and relayed the message. "What do I do now, James? Oh, I wish you were here! I need you."

"I wish I was there, too, but wishing doesn't erase the hundred miles that are between us. Call your mother. Call everybody you know and have them pray that Liz is okay. I'll call the church and have them set up a prayer chain."

"Will it work? Do you totally believe prayer will make everything okay?"

"I don't know, honey. I know God always answers and His answer is always what's best for us – but none of us ever knows what that answer will be."

She hung up the phone. The minute she did, she started sobbing uncontrollably. "Oh, please don't let Liz die," she cried in a loud, choked voice. "Please take care of her and the baby. Tom needs her. He loves her so much. Please, please don't let Liz die!"

She was going out to help in the search. There was no way she could stay put and not at least try to do something! Her phone rang before she could reach the door.

"Don't go out to look for her, Dani," James said.

How had he known what she was going to do? "James, I can't just sit here!"

"I've been watching the weather and I'm aware of the terrible storm there right now. I can hear it on the phone line. Honey, if you go out in it and you slide off the road or something, then you and Liz will both be in trouble. Please, promise me you won't go out."

She sniffed. "I won't go out. I love you, James."

"I love you, too."

She called her mother and told her what happened.

"Oh, dear, I'm so sorry!" Gina gasped. "Look, Rita and Roy are here. We'll all have a special prayer that everything is all right."

"You and Dad and...the Bakers...will pray?"

"Oh, yes, honey! You know Dad and I have always believed in prayer. Just recently, Rita and Roy have started attending church and they've become Christians. They'll be glad to join in the prayer."

Dani hung up the phone, trembling more than ever. Bits and pieces ran through her mind from the past – listening to Rita and Roy Baker talking, laughing and cursing. Yes, cursing - and cursing a lot. Rita and Roy shouting angry words at other family members, calling them names. They had never acted like Christians when she knew them eleven years ago. But when they were visiting her parents last week, they had been different. She hadn't paid any attention at the time, but now she realized how much calmer they'd been, how much more pleasant their conversation was. And there had been no cursing. Absolutely none. And Roy had said the table grace. Only now did she think about it. She couldn't help smiling. She was glad they had cleaned up their lives, especially when Rita was so sick. Was that what had led them to the Lord? Or had it happened before she became so ill?

The ringing phone jarred her out of her memory and she answered immediately without looking to see who was calling.

"Dani, Mom just told me about Liz. Is there anything I can do?"

It was Max. "There are several people out looking for her. Maybe you can help everybody pray."

Silence.

"She has to be all right, Max. She just has to be."

"I may not be much help with prayers, Dani, but I'm going out to help them search. She was my friend, too, you know."

Yes, she was. As Dani hung up the phone, she visualized Liz, Max and herself – together so many times, doing so many things. Liz would be with this boyfriend or that boyfriend, and she would always be with Max.

More tears fell. Tears for the loss of her first love. Tears for the tenderness and caring she'd just heard in Max's voice. Tears for Liz, for the terrible heartache she'd gone through with a guy she was sure she loved before she met Tom. But then came the smiles. One for the day she found James and one for when she fell head over heels in love with him. One for when Liz married Tom. One for their little baby, soon to be born.....

"Oh, God, you won't let anything happen to her or the baby. I just know it!"

The storm continued to rage as passing minutes seemed like hours and there was no news from Tom.   Dani paced the floor. She prayed. She cried. She called James over and over, just to hear his voice and to ask him to say another prayer.

What would she do without him? When she thought back to just a few short weeks ago and how she had started to doubt her love for him, she could hardly stand the guilt that surged through her body. Remembrance of the passionate kiss she'd shared with Max deepened it. Still, it had been that kiss that had opened her eyes to the truth of how much she truly did love her husband. Had it been one of the mysterious ways for which God was said to be famous?

The ringing of the phone shattered the moment and immediately her thoughts returned to Liz. When she saw Tom's number on the screen, she felt her heartbeat quicken.

"Tom?"

"We – found her. She had a flat tire and the car – the car ran off the road and into the creek." His voice broke.

"Is she all right? The baby?"

"She's being taken to the hospital right now. I'm following the ambulance."

"Is she all right?" Dani repeated, her voice shriller than before.

"I don't know. It – looks bad."

"I'm on my way to the hospital."

SIXTEEN

THEY ALL SAT IN THE WAITING ROOM TOGETHER – Liz and Tom's parents, Dani and Max – as Tom remained in the Emergency Room with his wife. No one spoke, but merely sat there in total silence, waiting, hoping and praying.

When Max reached over and took Dani's hand, she didn't pull away. Max loved Liz, too. He needed Dani's strength as much as she did his at the moment and she felt no threat from his touch.

"Nothing is going to happen to Liz or her baby," Max said, for about the hundredth time it seemed. "You gotta believe that, Dani. God wouldn't be that cruel."

Her eyes shiny with tears, she looked at him. "I know."

"I'm sorry," he then said in nearly a whisper.

Her eyes narrowed quizzically.

"For everything," he continued.

She didn't ask him what he meant. Somehow, she just knew. "I wish James was here."

"He would be if he could, you know."

"I know." A slight pause. "I'm sorry, too, Max."

He looked at her, waiting.

"For everything."

He squeezed her hand and stood up. "Want some coffee?"

"I would love some."

"Lots of cream and tons of sugar?"

She grinned. "You remembered."

"Some things you never forget."

"But some things change. I drink it black now. I decided all that cream and sugar I ingested when I was a teen ager was going to surely make me fat, so I cut it out."

He chuckled. "When you taste the coffee out of the machine in here, you might change your mind and want them put back in."   He turned and walked away.

She leaned back and closed her eyes for a moment, thinking of Liz and how she was fighting for not only her life but also the life of her child. If only she could turn back time. If she could just start the day over and never leave Liz alone. If she'd been there, Liz would've let her take her to wherever she needed to go.

She didn't expect to hear a small, still voice in her ear. A voice saying, "But you weren't there – because you need to be here right now to help pray Liz through this."

Her eyes popped open and she looked around the room. No one was standing over her. No one was speaking to her. Everyone was still sitting as quietly as before.

Her eyes stopped at the entranceway when the door opened and she gasped. It was the girl! How could she be here? Why was she here?

At first the young girl dressed in black didn't appear to see Dani, but when she did, she merely looked at her with no expression whatsoever. She didn't look surprised and neither smiled nor frowned. She just stood there, staring. Just as she'd done the other times.

Without hesitating, Dani stood up and walked over to her.

The girl never moved, but stood as still as a statue.

"Hello again," Dani said, smiling.

"I didn't expect to see you here."

"My friend was in an accident. We're all waiting for news."

"Oh."

That was it? That was all she was going to say? "Do you have somebody in here?"

"My mom's been here a long time. She's going to die here."

Dani's eyes widened. "Why do you say that?"

"No use lying about it. I gotta go." She started to turn away but Dani reached for her arm and stopped her.

"Please talk to me," she said. "I think you need to talk to somebody, so why not me?"

The girl smirked. "You're the last person I'd want to talk to. I said I gotta go." Jerking her arm roughly away, she turned and stormed back outside.

At the same time, Max returned. He looked at the disappearing figure of the young girl and then at Dani. "Who on earth was that? She looks like she's running for her life."

"I don't know who she is, but she might be doing that very thing, running for her life."

He handed her a cup of coffee and they walked together back to a seat and sat down. "She looked spooky to me," he said then, after he'd taken a sip of the hot liquid.

"I've seen her several times now and every time she was staring at me as if she either wanted to talk to me or kill me. I'm not sure which. This morning – oh, my gosh, was it only this morning? It seems like ages ago. Anyway, this morning, I met her. She lives in that trailer park just past where the woods that join my place ends is located."

"I know the place. It's creepy."

"Not creepy, just run down. The people there are poor, but that doesn't make them any different from any of the rest of us. It doesn't make them creepy." She took her first sip of coffee and made a face. "Ohh. You were right. I wish I had tons and tons of cream and sugar."

Laughing, he reached into his pocket and pulled out several packets of sugar and two individual creamers. "I told you. The creamer is French Vanilla."

She laughed, too. How ironic it was that Max always knew exactly what she would need. And exactly what flavor. Quickly, she brushed aside the thought. She hadn't meant it in the way it appeared in her mind.

"So who is she? What's her name?"

"She wouldn't tell me."

"I wonder why."

"She told me that someday I will know who she is and then I'll wish I didn't."

He screwed up his nose. "Weird."

"She told me just now that her mother is in this hospital and she's going to die here."

"Weirder yet."

She stirred the flavorings into the coffee and took another sip. "Much better now." Looking again at Max, "She's very pretty. If she were to smile, she'd be able to light up the room with her beauty."

"I didn't get that good of a look at her. All I saw was her fleeting back."

"I wonder how old she is. The first time I saw her, from a distance, I thought she might be 17 or 18, but now I think she might be a little older. Maybe even 20."

There was a moment of silence as they drank their coffee before Max spoke again. "Have you seen the nun again?" His eyes twinkled and she could tell he was trying very hard not to laugh.

"You can laugh all you want but I really did see her that day."

"I believe you."

"You do not."

"Yes, I do."

She recognized what he was doing. It was an old game they used to play, and she knew she had to stop it before it ended with the words they both spoke together: "Yes, I do – love you – with all my heart." She stood up. "I'm going to go see how all the parents are doing. They've been awfully quiet over there." She looked across the room to where Liz and Tom's mothers and fathers were sitting.

"You go on over and talk to them, Dani. I think I'll go outside for a while. I never did like hospitals."

She watched him leave with a heaviness in her heart. They'd spent the entire evening together in the waiting room, and aside from his making a joke or two every once in a while, Max hadn't said much at all. He wasn't like the Max she once knew – carefree, happy and always talking about something or other. Of course, this was neither the time nor place for idle chatter, she reminded herself. Still, for reasons she couldn't define, he seemed so very different. It saddened her because she knew the reason why.

He wasn't happy anymore.

SEVENTEEN

SOMETIME DURING THE NIGHT, after Max left and Tom and Liz's parents went to get something to eat, Dani fell asleep in the reclining chair in the waiting room.

"Dani." A soft voice caught her attention and she opened her eyes slowly. Who had spoken? Looking around her, she saw no one else in the room. In fact, she wasn't even in the waiting room any longer. She gasped at the realization. Where was she? Why was it so deathly quiet?

Something brushed against her arm. It was light like a feather and very soft. She saw nothing, except for puffy white clouds everywhere she looked. She felt the brushing sensation again and swiped at her arm, trying to make it stop.

Sudden laughter turned her deathly still. It was Liz! She was there with her. "Liz! Where are you? Why can't I see you?"

"Oh, Dani, you've been the best friend in the world to me and I love you so much. We'll see each other again, I promise you."

A wailing sound invaded the space and Liz laughed again. "Oh, that's my baby! He's so beautiful, Dani. You'll see him one of these days, I promise you."

A tear started slowly down Dani's cheek. "What do you mean, I'll see him one of these days? Liz, where are you? Why can't I see you and him now?"

"We're in heaven with Jesus! Oh, it's so beautiful here! Its way beyond anything I ever imagined. You'll see, Dani. One of these days, you'll see for yourself."

"You can't be in heaven! We need you here with us. Tom needs you. Liz, he would be lost without you. He can't make it without you and your son. Please come back!"

"Dani! Dani, wake up!"

She heard the voice, loud and clear, but couldn't manage to open her eyes. "Liz!" she called again.

"Dani!"

James? Was she hearing her husband's voice? Dani's eyes popped open, but for a moment all she could do was stare at him. He was standing over her, shaking her, calling her name, but he seemed so far away. Everything was fuzzy, his face, his voice.

"Dani! Are you all right? You must have been dreaming."

Dreaming. No, it wasn't a dream. It was so real. In that very instant, she came to herself. "James!" Jumping to her feet, she threw herself into his arms and started sobbing. "She's gone, James. Liz is dead and so is the baby and they are both in heaven!"

"Honey, honey….." He held her tightly against him, trying to soothe her. "You were dreaming."

"Dreaming? But - it was so real!" Her voice choked up again and she couldn't say anything more.

He continued to hold her, soothing her hair as he did, kissing her forehead, whispering consoling words.

She felt her body starting to calm but still she never let go of her fierce hold on him. The sobs subsided, turning into soft choking tears, then disappearing completely. Finally, she pulled back and looked into his eyes. "Oh, James! Oh, James, you're here!" It was as if she'd just realized he was standing there with her.

He kept smiling. "I left the minute I could get away. I couldn't let you go through this alone."

"I'm so glad you're here, but I wasn't alone. Both Tom and Liz's parents have been here the entire time, and Max."

"Max?"

"He and I and Liz were once all very good friends. He cares about her. He was with the search team when they found her."

"He was here with you – and I wasn't." James sighed.

"James....."

"I'm sorry. I'm glad you weren't alone. Really."

"Liz?"

"She's in surgery."

"Still?"

"I talked to Tom on the phone about a half hour ago, just before I got here.   All he could tell me was she was in surgery and – she was critical."

"She can't die. She just can't."

"How long has it been since you've eaten?"

"How could I even think of eating?"

"When this is all over, Liz might need you to help her out for a while. How can you help her if you don't eat and keep up your strength?"

She thought a moment. "You're right. I guess the last time I ate was at lunchtime. What time is it?"

"It's a little after midnight. We can run over to that all night diner across the street and have a sandwich."

"But I don't want to go anywhere."

"We'll just be across the street. We both have our phones. If anything happens, someone will call us."

She hesitated, then finally agreed to do as he wanted.

Sitting in a small booth in the diner a short time later, she told him about the dream she had. "It was so real. I couldn't see her, but I could hear her and I heard the baby crying. She told me they were both in heaven and someday I would see them. What if it was a premonition? What if she really is going to die?"

"We have to keep the faith. That's all we can do." He took a bite and chewed slowly, then took a sip of coffee. "I have something else I want to talk to you about, Dani. Maybe this is the right time and maybe it's not, but I've thought about it a lot lately, ever since Max came back into your life."

"Max isn't back in my life as anything more than a friend." It was on the tip of her tongue to confess everything that had happened since the first time she'd seen Max again. Didn't James have a right to know how emotional she'd been, and how it had actually wound up strengthening her love for him? "James....."

"No, don't say anything more. This is confession time for me."

Her eyes widened.

"I was upset when I found out about Max, especially when Tom confided in me about what Liz told him; that you and Max were more than close, that you were hopelessly in love and when he left you, you were devastated."

She waited.

"When I saw him, I couldn't help comparing the two of us. Here he was, at least 10 years younger, filled with vitality and handsome. I felt old and tired all of a sudden. You're so beautiful and so much younger. How could you not still be attracted to him?"

"James...."

"No, let me finish. What I'm trying to say is that I was scared to death of losing you to him, but then all of a sudden, you were more loving than ever. It should have made me feel better, but it heightened my insecurities. I wondered if all the extra love you were giving me was your way of trying your best to get over him, if you were pretending he was the one in your arms instead of me."

Tears welled in her eyes, but she said nothing.

"I love you more than my life, Dani. But if you decided you were no longer happy with me, that Max was the one and only one you could ever truly love, I – would let you go to him. I would never hold you, if you didn't want me."

She swallowed. "I love you, not Max."

He smiled deeply into her eyes. "Well, then, what do you say we put it all behind us and trust each other completely with our hearts?"

The ringing of his phone interrupted them and he answered at once. After a few seconds, he started to smile.

She breathed deeply, waiting. Was it about Liz?

"Liz is going to make it," he finally told her when he was off the phone. "That was Tom. She just got out of surgery. He said it was touch and go for quite a while, and at one time they thought they'd lost both her and the baby – but miraculously – they came back. She's going to be okay, and so is the baby. He's very tiny, but he's strong."

"Oh, thank God!" she cried.

EIGHTEEN

SHE COULDN'T BELIEVE IT!   When she and James walked into their home late Thursday afternoon, they found all the cabinet and pantry doors in the kitchen standing wide open. Going from one to another, they didn't find too much missing other than a few cans of soup, some crackers and some cereal. James checked the refrigerator.

"The burglar apparently likes cereal and milk, since there's very little cereal left and no milk at all," he said, unable to suppress a chuckle despite the circumstances.

Dani sat down at the table, saying nothing.

He sat down across from her. "What are you thinking?"

"I think we should wait up tonight and catch her in the act."

"Her?"

"The nun."

Again, he chuckled.

"Don't laugh at me. I saw her running."

"Be realistic, honey. You saw someone dressed in a long black dress and veil running into the woods. First of all, that doesn't mean she was running away from our house. Secondly, it doesn't mean she was a nun. It could've been anyone dressed in a long black dress and veil."

She sighed. "Would you like some coffee? Providing there is any in the canister."

Standing up again, he went to check. "She must not have been thirsty for coffee this time. It's still full." He went about the preparations of filling the carafe and spooning the coffee grounds into the filter, then flipped on the switch. "If she knew how expensive this coffee pot was, she'd probably have taken it by now." Again, he chuckled.

"Are you finished in Atlanta?"

He sat down again. "You want to change the subject."

"Yes."

"Yes, I am. Everything went like clockwork and we finished way ahead of schedule. How is your work load? Can we plan our vacation now?"

"We could, but….."

"But?"

"I want to go on a vacation. I really do. But, should we leave now? I mean, we need to find out for sure who is getting into the house and how they're doing it before we take off and leave everything to their disposal. Then there's Liz. I don't want to leave her right now."

"I hadn't planned to leave right away. It'll take some time to get everything set up." James smiled. "That baby is adorable, isn't he? Little Tommy Jr. What a head of hair for such a teeny, weeny thing."

She smiled, too. "I'm just so glad he's okay, even if he can't go home for a while. Maybe it's for the best. It'll give Liz some time for healing. Gosh, she was so lucky to have survived!"

"Everyone's calling it a miracle. After seeing that car a while ago, I believe it."

"She died and came back, James. I know she did. She came to talk to me and I told her how much Tom needed her and she came back."

"You still think she had a near death experience, like you told me at the hospital, and it wasn't simply your dream?"

"I do."

There was a moment of silence. When Dani looked over at her husband, his eyes seemed distant. "What are you thinking?"

"Uh – nothing."

"What kind of nothing?"

"I want a child, honey. Lately, I've been thinking of it a lot. I want one while I am young enough and have the strength and good health to enjoy it, play with it, and do things together."

She smiled. "So do I."

"You mean it?" He was standing up.

She stood up also, still smiling and welcomed the arms he closed around her.

He grinned. "It may take a while, I know, but that's okay. I don't mind it if it takes a little time and effort on our part. Do you?" He laughed and started nudging her across the room.

"What about the coffee?"

"It'll taste even better after a while."

THEY HAD JUST FINISHED DINNER when there was a loud knocking on the door.

"Who on earth can that be?" she asked as their quizzical gazes met.

"There's only one way to find out."

On the other side of the door stood their neighbor, Mary Narby, her eyes wide and frightened. "Oh, James! I'm so glad you're here. Look! The woods are on fire!"

His eyes followed hers. "Oh, no! Has anyone called the fire department?"

"I did, just before I came over."

As sirens sounded in the distance, James was running outside and quickly joining the crowd of onlookers who were gathering in the center of his yard. Dani followed, her eyes wide with shock and disbelief.

"I think somebody intentionally set it," said one elderly man named Mr. Doon.

"But why would anyone do that?" asked Miss Murray.

"Why does anyone do things they shouldn't do?" Mary Narby replied. "Somebody gets a grudge against you and burns down your woods. Thank goodness it wasn't a house."

'That's our woods,' thought Dani. 'We own that property!' As her eyes met James', she knew he was thinking the same thing.

Mr. Doon looked at James. "Somebody got something against you, James?"

Miss Murray sighed. "I don't see how anyone could have a grudge against either James or Dani. They're the best neighbors we've got."

Mary Narby frowned but didn't say anything.

"Well, it doesn't look like its spread much," put in another male neighbor. "Here comes the fire truck. Bet they can get it out in a minute."

The firefighters worked quickly and diligently to douse the flames. To everyone's relief, the fire was soon out, the crowd had disbursed and everyone went back to his own house.

Left alone, Dani and James walked to the edge of their yard to where the woods started. "This is scary."

"First we have a burglar, now someone tries to burn up the woods."

"So you think it was done on purpose, like Mr. Doon said?"

"I don't know what to think. What about you? Do you think your nun is responsible for this, too?"

"There's no way she would do such a thing!"

"But she would steal our food?"

"Perhaps she was hungry and had no choice. Somebody else set fire to the woods."

"I think the burglar and the arsonist are the same person. Let's go back inside now. It's getting cool out here."

She remained where she was. "I just thought of something."

He waited.

"The fire was contained to such a small area that it must have been started very recently. I mean, if it would've been started earlier, it would have spread much further. If we look around a little, we might find some sort of clue that could lead to whoever did this."

"If you'll notice, they've restricted the area until the ones who are trained in the field can investigate it. That's what all this yellow tape is for, to keep everybody else out."

"But it's our land. They can't keep us off it."

"If we start stomping around in there, we might do more harm than good. We might cover up any evidence, rather than uncover it."

She sighed. "I guess you're right."

NINETEEN

WHO COULD'VE SET THE FIRE AND WHY? Dani lie in bed, her eyes wide and sleepless while her husband snored softly beside her. What if Mary Narby was right, if someone did have some kind of grudge against them and was seeking revenge? She couldn't think of any enemies they might have. She and James were personable and friendly, minded their own business, and as far as she could tell everyone they knew liked them. It could be someone they didn't know. People were known to terrorize total strangers. The thought made her shudder. Were she and her husband simply somebody's random target?

Her thoughts switched from the fire to the burglaries, then to Liz's accident, to Max, and finally to the mysterious young girl who was perpetually angry.

She rolled over, trying to shut off her thoughts and go to sleep. What time was it anyway? Glancing at the illuminated numbers on the bedside clock, she groaned inwardly. Only eleven o'clock? They hadn't gone to bed until ten. Had it only been one hour?

She decided to get up for a while. Maybe if she listened to some soft music or watched some TV, she'd get sleepy. She hated nights like this. Ordinarily, she had no trouble sleeping, but on the rare occasions that she had a case of insomnia, it truly irritated her.

She made her way to the kitchen. There was always a small night light on over the stove, so she didn't stop to turn on any more. She didn't want to be in enough brightness to wake her up even more. Her small radio was sitting on the counter and she turned it on, reducing the volume to very low. She wished she liked milk. Everyone always said warm milk would make you sleepy. Just the thought of it was nauseating. Maybe some hot cocoa would help.   She often drank that. In a few minutes, she had fixed a cup and sat down by the table to drink it.

Again, she started thinking about the fire. What if it had started at night, instead of the early evening, and no one had seen it right away? If everyone had been sleeping, how far might it have spread? Their little shed housing their lawn supplies, riding mower and gasoline wasn't far away. Gasoline. If the fire had reached those gasoline cans.......

She forced her mind to stop. "I can't keep worrying about this. It didn't happen. Nothing was hurt. Everyone is safe. I should be thanking the Lord, instead of sitting here delighting the devil with all my fears."

But how did she shut off her mind? Standing up, she left the kitchen and went to her office. There was a program on the computer that referenced Bible scriptures. Maybe she could look up some on fear.

In just a few moments, she had a list of passages that talked about fear. She started looking them up and reading them aloud.

"There is no fear in love; but perfect love casteth out fear: because fear hath torment. He that feareth is not made perfect in love. Ye shall not fear them: for the LORD your God he shall fight for you. And he saith unto them, Why are ye fearful, O ye of little faith? Then he arose, and rebuked the winds and the sea; and there was a great calm. For God hath not given us the spirit of fear; but of power, and of love, and of a sound mind."

She was amazed. There were dozens and dozens of verses about fear. It made it very plain that a person should never give in to it, but should always trust God when fear tried to overpower them.

She bowed her head. "Help me, Father. Help me to not be afraid and help me to fully and completely believe. Erase any doubts that have bothered me lately about the Bible stories. Yes, they do seem impossible to our limited human minds, but with God, all things are possible. Aren't they?"

A verse she'd read, perhaps years ago, popped into her mind, and she spoke it aloud. "Lord, I believe. Help thou mine unbelief."

A yawn escaped her and she smiled. She knew what to do the next time she couldn't sleep. Just talk to God about it for a while.

In her bed again, she fell asleep immediately and never opened her eyes until the sun was shining through the window. Rolling over, she noticed James was gone. She hoped he hadn't left for work yet so they could have coffee together. The clock said 7:30. He should still be home.

He was sitting at the table scanning the newspaper and looked up at her when she entered the kitchen. "Good morning!"

She smiled, walked over and kissed him. "I'm so glad you're still here."

"I'll be here all day."

Her eyes widened. "You aren't going to work?"

"Nope. Since the Atlanta job is finished, I'm taking a few days off. I placed ad for a couple more techs, too, so I can take more time off. What about you? You aren't going to have to sit at that computer the whole time I'm off, are you?"

She poured herself some coffee and sat down across from him. "I have one assignment that I'm nearly finished with and I'm not accepting any more for a while. I need a reprieve, too. All I really want to do today is go visit Liz. No telling how long she'll have to stay in the hospital. I'm so glad you're staying home." She went on to tell him about her sleepless night. "I was worried about everything. You name it, I was worried about it. But you know what? I looked up scriptures on fear and then I prayed. Then I went back to bed and slept like a baby."

He smiled. "You should've woke me. I'd have read them with you."

She grinned. "If I'd woke you, you might have been grumpy because you were sleepy."

"Right now I'm grumpy because I'm hungry. Let's fix up a big breakfast."

"How about some pancakes and sausage?"

"With an egg on the side?"

She giggled softly, stood up and went to the pantry. "One pancake mix." Next was the refrigerator. "Some milk and some.......oughto!"

He looked at her quizzically.

"There's no eggs."

Their eyes met. They both knew there had definitely been eggs in the refrigerator when they went to bed.

"I was up til after midnight," she said. "She had to come after that."

"Or before you got up the first time."

"I got up a little after eleven. I didn't look in the refrigerator then. Well, I did. I got out some milk to make some hot chocolate, but I didn't pay attention to whether or not there were any eggs."

"But we definitely knew there were eggs when we went to bed because we had egg salad sandwiches for supper."

She sighed. "Why does she keep doing this?"

"Maybe you're right about what you suggested last night."

Her eyes met his quizzically.

"Maybe we should sit up and wait for – her – to come. We'll get comfortable, in the dark, and nab – her- when she comes through the door."

She grinned, very much aware of the emphasis he put on the word 'her'. "And it will finally prove to you that it really is just a hungry nun."

He grinned back. "Or not."

TWENTY

IT WAS ALL DANI COULD DO to keep from crying when she looked at Liz, lying in the hospital bed with her leg in a cast, bandages around her chest and her face all bruised and swollen. "I'm so sorry you're hurt," she said softly. "I wish I could take it all away."

Liz smiled, then grimaced. "It'll go away. I'm just thankful to be alive."

Dani placed the bouquet of flowers she'd brought on the window ledge, then sat down in a chair near Liz's bed. "What can I do for you? Anything you need, just say the word and I'll get it for you."

"I have everything I need. I have a wonderful husband and the most beautiful baby. Have you seen him yet, Dani? He's the most beautiful baby in the world."

Dani smiled. "Of course he is. How could he not be when he has the most beautiful mother in the world?"

"Is James with you?"

"He had something else to do. He'll come by later." She didn't mention that he was meeting with the sheriff to discuss the fire and the latest of the burglaries. There was no point in even mentioning the fire to her friend, even though she already knew about the missing food. There was no need to upset her about anything. She had enough to worry about.

Dani smiled again. "Since he's seen little Tommy, he really, really wants a baby of his own."

Liz chuckled, then as she'd done before, grimaced afterward from the pain. "So?"

Dani laughed. "So do I."

"This makes me so happy! Dani, if you have a little girl, maybe she and Tommy will get married someday."

"My goodness, Liz! I'm not even pregnant yet and you already have my daughter getting married!"

"Well, Tommy's got such dark hair and your little girl will probably be blonde like you, so just think of the beautiful children you'll have."

"Now you're making me a grandmother."

They laughed together.

Liz flinched.

"Don't try to laugh anymore," Dani said. "It's hurting you too much. Do you want some water or anything? Ice?"

"I just want to hold my baby. I can't even go to the nursery to see him yet. Tom's been there and he's brought me some pictures but it's not the same. I can't wait til I can get out of this bed."

"Liz, do you remember anything strange that happened while you were in surgery?"

Liz's eyes became quizzical. "Strange? I don't remember anything from the time I left the store until I woke up after the surgery. Why do you ask?"

"I was – just wondering."

"No, you have a reason. You always have a reason for your questions."

"It's okay. We'll talk about it when you feel better."

"Come on, Dani. Tell me now."

"Tom said you flat-lined once."

"Oh! That! He said it was around midnight."

"That's what he told us." It had been midnight when James had awakened her from her dream. She had to know if it really was a dream or a near death experience. She wouldn't prompt Liz to say anything. She'd just wait and see if her friend remembered, if it truly might have happened.

Liz was quiet for what seemed a very long time. For a while, she stared at the ceiling, then she closed her eyes and opened them again, as if she was in deep thought. Then she began to speak in a very soft voice. "I can't remember. Has someone told you something that I should remember?"

"No." Dani stood up. "You're really tired. I'm going to go now, but I'll be back tomorrow. If you need me for anything before then, have somebody call me. I don't care if it's the middle of the night. Let me know. Promise?"

"I promise. And I'll think on your question. If the Lord wants me to remember something, He will."

Dani kissed her friend's forehead and smoothed her dark hair back from it. "I love you."

"I love you, too. So hurry up and get pregnant so we can be grandmothers together."

They both laughed. Liz flinched. Dani left.

Outside the doorway, Dani stopped for a moment. If Liz truly did have a near death experience, would she ever remember it? She wanted so much to know if it truly happened, or of she'd merely had a dream, as James kept trying to convince her.

She walked down the hallway. At the nursery window, she stopped and looked in, her eyes roving until she caught sight of little Tommy's incubator. She smiled as she watched him kicking his little feet and moving his tiny arms. He was crying, too. What a wail from such a little fellow! A nurse walked over to him and touched him, soothing him immediately. When the nurse looked up, she spotted Dani and smiled at her. Dani smiled back and walked on down the hall way. She was like Liz. She couldn't wait until she could hold that baby in her own arms! And she couldn't wait until she could hold her own baby in her own arms! Remembering the conversation just now with Liz about being grandmothers together made her chuckle. What a beautiful thought!

She had just reached the waiting room and started to open the door to go outside when she saw her. The young girl dressed in black. She was sitting in a far corner of the room with her head in her hands. Her body was shaking. Even from as far away as she was, Dani knew she was crying.

Should she go to her? Could she be a comfort to her or would it irritate her to see her again? For some reason, the girl didn't seem to like Dani at all. Dani hesitated, wondering what to do. Had her mother died?

She knew she would never forgive herself if she didn't offer comfort, whether the girl accepted it or not. Walking over to her, she touched her arm lightly.

The girl jumped and looked up. Immediately, she wiped her eyes with her sleeve.

Uninvited, Dani sat down next to her. "Can I help you? Is your mother worse?"

The girl swallowed and looked away.

"My name's Dani," Dani volunteered.

"Weird name for a female," she mumbled.

"It's really Danita, but everybody always calls me Dani. Except my mother. She refuses to use anything but my given name." She smiled.

The girl said nothing, but kept looking at the floor the entire time Dani was talking.

"Are you hungry?" Dani asked then. "Can I get you something?"

"Why do you always think I must be hungry? I have plenty to eat."

After a moment of silence, Dani spoke again. "Is there anything I can do for you? Can I say a prayer for you?" She'd never asked anyone that question before and it surprised her when it rolled so easily off her lips. She'd always had trouble praying aloud. What would she do if the girl accepted?

"No prayers."

Another short silence. "What's your name?"

The girl's eyes met hers and Dani could clearly see the anger in them. "If I wanted you to know my name, I would've told you, *Danita*." She emphasized Dani's name.

"I'd like to be your friend, if you'll let me."

The girl smirked. "You don't want to be my friend, believe me, and you never will be." Jumping to her feet, she nearly ran in an effort to get away from her.

Dani stared after her, thoroughly confused. Something was bothering that girl. Not only bothering her, it was eating her up. Did she have anyone to confide in, or was she carrying a heavy burden all by herself? Every time she'd seen her, she'd been alone. Again, she wondered if her mother had died. She'd told Dani the other night that she would die in the hospital. Who was her mother? Perhaps Dani could find her and talk to her. There must be some way she could help this girl!

She didn't know why she was so determined to do it. She just knew she had to! As she stood up, she saw the girl again. She was stopped in the hallway, talking to a doctor.

Dani watched, waiting until the girl walked on down the hallway and was out of sight and then walked up to the same doctor.

"I wonder if you can help me," she asked him.

He was an older man, with soft graying hair and grey eyes that twinkled when he smiled at her. "You're Dani, aren't you? Liz Grant's friend."

Only then did she recognize him as the doctor who had been in the ER when Liz was brought in. It surprised her that he'd remember her, with all the confusion. She smiled. "Yes, I am. You remember me."

"It's not easy to forget a beautiful face like yours." He laughed. "Now, how can I help you, Dani?"

"That young girl that was just talking to you. She looks so familiar to me but I can't remember her name."

"She has a name as beautiful as your face. Sorry, I don't mean to embarrass you but when you're my age you need to throw out compliments freely."

She couldn't help liking him. "A beautiful name?"

"Yes. Her name is Star. Star Light."

Dani's eyes became confused. "Her name is Starlight?"

"It's both her names. Her first name is Star and her last name is Light."

"Wow! That's hard to believe."

"It's the truth."

"Do you know anything about her?"

"Probably no more than you do, other than her name."

"She said her mother is in here and she's very sick."

The doctor's eyes widened. "Oh? If the two of you have been conversing, why didn't you ask her what her name was? Why ask me instead?"

Dani sighed. "I did. She wouldn't tell me."

He waited for her to continue.

"Do you know her mother? Can you tell me who she is and what room she's in?"

"I'm sorry, Dani, I really don't know. I retired from practice some time ago and have been filling in at the emergency room temporarily. The young girl, Star, came in this morning with a minor injury. I'm not free to discuss it, of course. That's all I know about her, her name."

"But you were just talking to her!"

His eyes twinkled again. "So were you."

TWENTY-ONE

Aʟʟ ᴅᴜʀɪɴɢ ʜᴇʀ ꜱᴇᴠᴇʀᴀʟ ᴠɪꜱɪᴛꜱ ᴛᴏ ᴛʜᴇ ʜᴏꜱᴘɪᴛᴀʟ to see Liz the next week, Dani never saw Star Light again. Still concerned for her and wanting to talk to her mother, Dani finally went to the information desk and inquired about what room Mrs. Light was in, only to discover there was no one there by that name. Had Star been lying? It occurred to her that Star might not have the same last name. Maybe she was married. There were any number of reasons why her name could be different. Then again, since Star hadn't been there lately, maybe her mother had made a turn for the better and gone home. Or died.

She tried to put the girl out of her mind. Often, she succeeded but sooner or later the thoughts of her would come back. Why couldn't she stop worrying about her? It was apparent Star didn't want anything to do with her, nor did she want her help. Just the same, Dani found herself whispering Star's name over and over during her prayers.

She and James were both happy when their food stopped disappearing. When their new security system was finally installed, they were sure that was one problem that was over with and done.

Just the same, she couldn't help wondering about the nun. Why hadn't she come back before the new system was in? Dani was certain that no one else believed it could be a nun who was responsible. Even to her own mind, it seemed impossible, but she had seen her with her own eyes. Was she getting food someplace else now or was she going hungry?

There she went, worrying again. She worried when the food disappeared and she worried when it didn't!

She was sitting at her vanity, fixing her hair on Thursday morning, a week after Liz's accident, and her thoughts were running rampant. James was gone and the house was so quiet. Too quiet, she decided. It gives me too much time to think.

The fire in the woods was still a complete mystery. After a thorough search, other than discovering it had definitely been arson, there had been no kind of evidence as to who was responsible. Why would anyone do such a thing? What if they tried again?

She shook her head, trying to ward off the fear that accompanied the questions of her mind.

Then she thought of Max. She hadn't seen him since the day of the accident, but Liz mentioned he'd been in to visit her a couple times. She hoped he'd find some new happiness in his life. Even though he'd been responsible for their break up so many years ago, she no longer harbored any anger against him. They were young. She lived through her tears and met the most wonderful man in the world later on. How could she resent Max for that?

She finally stood up and went to her bureau for her favorite tee shirt. It surprised her that it wasn't on the top of the stack, where she always put it, but then she remembered James had put some clothes away for her the other day and that was probably why. Rooting around in search of it, her fingers touched a folded piece of paper on the very bottom. She pulled it out. It was the note. She'd forgotten all about it. Opening it up, she read again the small, dark letters.

"He owes me all. I owe him nothing. Keep this between us and all I'll ever do is take a few essentials that should be mine anyway. Tell the Starrman and I might tell him a thing or two about you and your boyfriend."

The words still puzzled her as much as they had before. A sudden thought struck her. Had James seen it when he'd put the clothes away? No, he couldn't have. He would have said something, asked her about it. James wasn't a person to keep quiet if he was concerned about something, no matter what it was.

Unlike her and the fact that she was still harboring the secret of the passionate, forbidden kiss between her and Max in the woods that day.

With a deep sigh, she looked beneath the second shirt on the stack and found the one she was looking for. There was no way James could've seen the note on the very bottom. Stashing it back into the same spot, she closed the drawer, put on the shirt and started for her office.

She was going to confess everything to her husband. She couldn't keep worrying about what would happen if he found out on his own.

Right now, she had a story to work on, a deadline to meet.

Were Adam and Eve sorry for their sin against God? Staring at the blank screen of her computer, she pondered the thought. How might they have really felt about what they'd done after they lost everything because of it?

This was to be a follow-up to the story she'd done on the first man and woman a couple weeks ago. Closing her eyes, she forced herself to think deeply on the subject, for some scriptures to reference – but nothing came to her. "Help me, Lord," she whispered. "Help me to show others that all things really do work together for good, even the very worst sin ever committed."

It occurred to her suddenly how much she'd been praying lately. The thought brought a smile. Just in the last couple of weeks, she'd felt led to pray more often than she ever had. So much had happened, and every bit of it was something else to trust the Lord to handle.

So....back to Adam and Eve.....

Very unexpectedly, a vision filled her mind. It was so vivid she could have sworn she was sitting in a movie theatre, watching a large cinema screen.

A young couple was standing beneath a copse of trees laden with lush, thick dark green leaves. Behind them was a brilliant blue sky and surrounding them were what looked like a thousand more trees. At first, all they did was stand silently, looking all around them, but then he turned to her and took her in his arms.

Dani shivered, actually feeling the love between them. It seemed to be radiating everywhere and not just within their bodies. It was in the sweetness of the air, the beauty of the trees, and swirling around as if by magic within the blades of the green grass and the silvery blue waters of the sea. The depth of it created such an intense aura of brightness that everything sparkled, shimmered and glistened like millions of diamonds. It could not only be seen, it could also be felt. Like gentle fingers teasing tender skin. Like a soft breath of warm air wafting through the silence of a perfectly still night. And it could be heard. There was also music. No words, just a soft, sweet rhythm that permeated throughout everything – the sea, the grass and the sky. Never was there such a lovely, exotic sound.

Then the man spoke. Even though his lips didn't move, his words could be heard plainly and clearly. "We have lost everything, Eve, but we have found something magical. Love."

She smiled at him, a smile that radiated her entire countenance. "God's love. He always knew It would all work out for good, didn't He, Adam? He knew if we'd never tasted the forbidden fruit, we would never have known this beautiful love we now have for Him – and for each other."

"It was no accident. I believe it was all according to His plan. We knew from the beginning He loved us, but if it hadn't happened as it did, would we have known the true depth of His love? If everything in our lives had remained perfect and we had everything we ever wanted without having to work for it, would we have truly seen a need to depend upon God? Would we have deeply desired His love if we already had it, with no effort of our own to get it?" He paused a moment. "I'm sorry we disobeyed, but I'm glad to know He continues to love us anyway.   I have no fear of what lies beyond tomorrow, although I am saddened that future generations will have to suffer because of what we did."

"And God will have to come up with a plan to redeem the entire world. I fear that great pain and injustice will be the result of it."

"But the pain will be created because of love."

"And that love will bring many to believe in God."

As quickly as it had come, the vision was gone.

"Oh, my goodness!" Dani cried aloud. "I have to write this down before I forget it!"

Her fingers flew so quickly over the keys she could hardly see them move. When she finished, she reread her words and smiled.

"The Lord really *does* work in mysterious ways," she said aloud. "I never imagined the sin of Adam and Eve as being a part of God's plan for all of our lives. I always looked at it as their big mistake, but if they hadn't done it, would anyone have ever known the true depth of God's love? He loved them, despite their faults. Even when He couldn't let them stay in the beautiful garden, He still loved them. I believe He was with them all the days of their lives – and He will be with us throughout ours, too."

I believe. The words repeated themselves in her mind. Yes, she did believe – truly and completely. She didn't need some great explanation to prove that the Bible was true and so were the stories within it. All she needed as total and absolute proof – was to believe it!

Her excitement mounted, as she said over and over, "I believe! I believe! I believe!"

The sudden ringing of her phone shattered the revered silence surrounding her. At first, she sighed, wishing it hadn't happened when it did. When she looked to see who was calling and saw her mother's name and number, she answered quickly.

"How are you, dear?" Gina Cabot asked.

"I just finished an incredible story, Mom."

"Your stories are all incredible. I have every one of them, you know."

"No, I didn't know."

"I'm your mother. Why wouldn't I? But the reason I am calling is that Rita Baker has taken a severe turn for the worse. Roy wants to take her to the hospital but she insists she'll die once she goes there and she wants to stay alive as long as she can."

She felt sorry for Rita. No matter what happened between them, she loved her at one time and still did. She waited for Gina to continue.

"She's gotten very adamant about wanting to talk to you, Dani. Her husband, apparently, knows what it's about and has tried to talk her out of it, but she's insisting she has to tell you something before she dies."

"Mom....."

"There's no time to waste. You really must go see her. Don't call her on the phone. Go talk to her in person."

Dani sighed. "I don't understand any of this. What in the world could be bothering her that involves me? Okay. I'll drive over."

"Thank you, dear. Please do it quickly, today if you can."

With a deep sigh, she hung up the phone. "Well, Lord, it seems there might be another challenge ahead."

TWENTY-TWO

AFTER THE VISIT, Dani drove home in a daze. What Rita told her was shocking and unbelievable. Knowing Rita as well as she had all those years ago, she would never have imagined Max's mother could have done what she had. Nor would she have believed that Max would go along with it. That was what hurt the most.

She told her husband about it as they were relaxing on the sofa in the living room after dinner. "She told me that Max didn't break up with me because he'd found somebody else. She was concerned about how serious we were becoming and afraid he'd give up the prestigious career they had planned for him by rushing into marriage. They gave him an ultimatum. If he didn't let me go, they would disinherit him."

James listened silently.

"They told him they would not pay for his college or help him in any way because they knew it would be a waste of money. He'd be so involved with a wife, and maybe a child much too quickly, that he'd probably flunk out and they'd lose everything."

He never said a word, but watched her every expression. How did this news affect her feelings for Max, now that she knew he hadn't left her for someone else but that he was forced to do it by his parents?

She met his eyes. "I can't believe they would do it, James. Even more, I can't believe Max agreed to it, that he even lied to me about there being somebody else in the picture. He was so convincing. He even cried, because he didn't want to hurt me."

He finally spoke. "So how are you feeling about it, now that you know? Do you see Max in a different light? Do you feel sorry for him for the choice he was forced to make – either his career or you?"

"I feel…..angry! I was devastated when he told me he didn't love me anymore, but I could finally accept it because I knew he hadn't meant for it to happen. But he lied! If he loved someone else, it wasn't his fault. Love makes its own choices. But he didn't have anyone else. He just didn't love me enough to choose me when it came down to the nitty gritty. If he'd really, truly loved me, nothing could have made him do what he did."

"What I can't understand is why Rita is telling you all this now. If she's as sick as you said, why didn't she just let dead dogs lie and take it to the grave with her?"

"She said she had to have my forgiveness, that all this has been eating her alive ever since she became a Christian."

"So what did you tell her?"

"I told her it was in the past, that it was over and done and that I wished she'd never said anything about it."

He waited.

"Is forgiveness that important?"

"Forgiveness is very important. The Bible plainly tells us that if we don't forgive others, neither will God forgive us. Forgiveness gives freedom not only to the one who is being forgiven, but also to the one giving it."

She was silent for a very long time before she spoke again. "What are you thinking about this?"

"Why do you ask that? This is about you, not me."

"No, it concerns both of us. I don't want you to think that this makes a difference in the way I feel for Max now. In a way, I guess it does but not in how you might think. Instead of making me care more for him, it makes me……it makes me almost hate him."

"Hate's a very strong word, honey. My mother used to tell me all the time to never hate anyone. You can hate their ways, she'd say, but you should never hate the person himself."

"So I hate what he did. He hurt me so badly!"

"Maybe he's another one you'll have to forgive."

"He hasn't asked for forgiveness! I'm sure he has no idea that his mother has told me all this stuff."

"And maybe he never will, but you will never have true peace if you don't forgive him anyway."

Suddenly, she smiled. "You know what?"

"What?"

"None of this matters now. If he hadn't broke up with me, we may have gotten married and been totally unhappy. Because he did break up with me, I found you and I can't imagine myself ever being married to anyone else."

He grinned. "I like the sound of those words." He pulled her close and kissed her lips gently.

The kiss quickly deepened and became passionate.

Until she pushed him away. "James…"

He didn't answer but simply looked deeply and lovingly into her eyes.

"I want you to know, beyond the shadow of a doubt, that I love you with all my heart. But I need to tell you something."

"Honey," he whispered, nibbling on her ear, "can confession time wait a little while?"

"I'm afraid it's waited long enough. Something happened that you need to know, that I never had the nerve to tell you."

He waited.

"The day Max came by and we went into the woods together to try to find the nun I'd seen……" She stopped, wishing her heart would slow down.

He never said a word.

"He kissed me."

He swallowed. "And?"

"I – I kissed him back. Urgently and passionately."

He let go of her as if she'd suddenly burned him.

Her eyes welled with tears. "I was so emotional when I saw him again. I felt like Eve in the garden, staring at that forbidden fruit. I wanted a taste of it so badly that I couldn't think of anything else."

His eyes showed hurt, then anger. "So what else did you do, Dani?"

"I wanted more and so did he, but…..thank God, my senses came rushing back and I pushed him away. It was in that moment, after that stolen piece of intimacy and giving in to the forbidden, that I knew for sure that it was you I was in love with, you I wanted – and that it was all over with Max."

He stood up and walked across the room, stopping to look out the window. Then he turned back to her again. "Why are you telling me now? Why not just keep it as a secret in your own heart, like you thought Rita should've done with hers?"

"Maybe, like Rita, I knew I had to be truthful and need your understanding and forgiveness."

A long, painful silence ensued, during which time James paced back and forth across the floor and Dani continued to sit on the sofa, watching him.

"There's something else," she said then.

He waited.

"The – person – who has been taking our food left a note. That's the real reason I went to stay with my parents' while you were in Atlanta the first time."

"And you're just now telling me? What's going on?"

"I couldn't tell you before because – because I had to tell you about that day in the woods first. She saw us. After Max left, I asked God to forgive me and she plainly told me God didn't hear prayers from people like me. I never saw her but I heard her. Then....I got the note. She threatened to tell you what she saw. I was afraid she'd add a lot more to it than actually happened. I wanted you to know the truth, from my lips – but I've been too afraid to tell you."

"All this time? It's been over three weeks!"

"She knows your name."

"What?"

"On the note, she said she'd tell the Starrman about me and my boyfriend."

"This is crazy!"

"You have to believe me. I'm not lying about any of this."

"What did you do with the note?"

"It's in my bureau drawer."

"So the note's the real reason you haven't been very upset about the missing food. You were being blackmailed."

"I didn't think of it that way, but I guess you're right." Standing up, she walked over to him. "Please forgive me. I can't stand it if you don't."

He simply said, "Let me see the note. You know we could've used it as evidence. There might be some fingerprints on it."

She started across the room, praying with every step that her husband would quickly remember his own words of just moments ago about forgiveness.

Silently, he followed her.

TWENTY-THREE

HE WENT TO BED EARLY, feigning extreme tiredness. Without as much as a good night kiss or hug, he simply disappeared into their bedroom and closed the door behind him.

She watched with tears in her eyes. Had she done the right thing in telling him the truth?

She went back to her computer and reread the last story she'd written. It didn't seem nearly as exciting or interesting as it had before. So what if the sin of Adam and Eve did begin the chain of true love. It also created heartache and pain.

After nearly a half hour of sitting there and staring at her screen, she stood up and went to the kitchen. Turning on her radio, she fixed herself a cup of hot chocolate and sat down at the table. Would things ever be the same between her and James again? Or would he never fully trust her again?

When the phone rang, she answered quickly.

It was Liz. "Oh, Dani, I finally remembered what happened during my surgery!"

She perked up immediately. "I'm listening."

"I had a near death experience! I know I did. Oh, I know some people don't believe in them, and I'm not sure I did myself up until now. Can you talk now? It's not a bad time, is it?"

A bad time? It was the best time in the world. Just the sound of her best friend's voice was uplifting, not to mention what she was actually saying. "We can talk all night if we want to. James has already gone to bed."

"To bed? But it's only 9:00!"

"He was tired. He had a difficult day." Brought on by her confession, but she couldn't tell Liz that.

"Anyway, I did die! I remember being in a great deal of pain. Then I closed my eyes and suddenly all the pain was gone! I felt like I was light as a feather! Then I saw myself floating over the surgical table. I was holding Tommy in my arms and he was looking all around, like he was seeing everything that was happening. It never occurred to me that I might be dead, and if I was, my baby was, too. All I knew was that I felt so good and so peaceful and so happy. Not a pain anywhere!"

Dani waited as Liz paused and took in a deep breath.

"Then, I saw this bright light and I started toward it. I heard it speak and I knew it was Jesus in that light. He told me to look down. I didn't want to look down. I didn't want to look anywhere but at Him! But He told me again to look down, and I did. I saw you, Dani! Did you hear me? I saw you!"

"Yes, I hear you!"

"I thought I tried to tell you how happy I was and that I was in heaven with Jesus. Then Tommy started to cry. I didn't know why he would cry when he was so happy a moment before. And then I heard you telling me I had to come back, that Tom needed me. That's when I saw him, my husband. He was crying in wrenching sobs and his whole body was shaking. And he was praying. I can still hear him praying with all his heart for God to let me live." Liz sniffed and stopped talking.

Dani waited, swallowing her own tears.

"Then Jesus looked at me through that bright light and He asked me if I wanted to go back. I didn't want to, Dani! But then I heard your words again and I heard Tom crying. And I told Jesus I wanted to be with my husband."

There was a long silence as they cried together over the phone.

"Is that what you wanted me to remember?" Liz asked. "How did you know?"

"I knew you were there with me. I couldn't see you but I heard you talking and I heard Tommy crying. James has tried to convince me that I was dreaming, but I wasn't. Now I know I wasn't!"

"This is just so overwhelming! Just imagine, Jesus actually giving me a choice as to whether to live or die! I gotta go now. I'm exhausted, and I want to get a really good night's sleep tonight. I might get to go home tomorrow, you know. Oh, I can hardly wait."

"Me, too. Bye, Liz."

"Give James a big hug and kiss for me. And, you two hurry up and get that baby started!" She laughed and hung up the phone.

Dani smiled, but at the same time, she cried. There was one thing she hadn't told her husband yet, the fact that she had taken a home pregnancy test that morning – and it was positive. She hadn't planned to say anything until she'd seen her doctor, just in case the reading had been wrong.

Would the news be as exciting to him now as it would have been before?

Did she do the right thing by telling him the truth about Max?

Restless and knowing there was no way she could sleep, she took her cup of hot chocolate and went outside to sit on the porch. Swinging slowly back and forth on the glider, she tried to clear her mind of all her misgivings.

Soon, she found herself captivated by her surroundings. The moon was partially full and illuminated at least half of the yard, leaving the rest in darkness to create a mystical effect. Watching it, she couldn't help smiling. Who wouldn't want to smile when viewing the beauty of God's handiwork? After a few minutes, she stood up and left the porch and started walking through the soft green grass. The night air was warm and sweet-smelling and she breathed in deeply several times, enjoying the savor of it. New buds were bursting forth on the tree branches silhouetted against the dark sky. It was a beautiful evening. If only James were there with her, she would be completely happy and contented.

Suddenly, she stopped in her tracks. She could swear she'd heard something near the area of their little tool shed at the edge of the yard. Standing very still, she waited. Perhaps it had simply been her imagination, which had a habit of running rampant lately. No, it was real. It happened again and she could just barely make out the moving image of someone carrying a small flashlight approaching the door.

Shielding herself from view by standing behind a tree, she watched as the person seemed to be struggling with the lock. He was trying to break in! Her heart began to race wildly as she wondered what in the world she could do to stop him. If she went inside to get James, her movement would more than likely be seen beneath the sliver of the moon and whoever it was would get away. Or attack her. She shivered, becoming even more frightened.

If only she had her phone with her. Very rarely was she without it, but this was one of those times.

Her attention was quickly drawn back to the intruder. He was opening the door. Somehow, he had managed to pry the lock and he was looking inside, flashing the light all around in front of him. Then he went in.

An inner voice screamed within her. "You can't just stand here and let somebody steal everything you have! You've got to do something!"

She was too frightened to move even a muscle. Even though he was now inside the building and wouldn't be able to see her, she found she couldn't move an inch from the spot where she was hiding. All she could do was continue to watch, expecting him to push out the expensive lawn mower or any of the other tools that were inside.

He was coming out again. Her eyes widened when she saw what he had. It was the gasoline can! He set it on the ground and opened it, then started pouring it out onto the ground. He was going to set a fire!

No! God, help!

He was reaching inside his pocket and taking something out, something small. A cigarette lighter?

"No! Stop! Get out of here at once!" Her words were real and loud as she shouted out a warning. "I'll shoot. I swear I will!"

The stunned intruder stopped in his tracks, then turned and fled to the edge of the woods, disappearing immediately.

"Oh, God! Oh, God!" Still paralyzed to the spot by her fear, Dani felt as if she was surely going to faint. Instead she started screaming at the top of her lungs. "James! James! Help!"

There was no sound from inside the house. Could she make him hear her? She tried again to move, but couldn't. Never had she been so frightened in her entire life. "James!" She screamed again, this time louder than ever. "James! Help!"

A light came on from inside the house.

Sighing with relief, she called his name again.

The porch light came on and he ran outside, barefooted and wearing only his pajama bottoms. "Dani! Dani, where are you?" His voice sounded every bit as terrified as hers, as he leapt down the steps and ran into the yard.

"Over here!" Overcome by relief at just seeing him, she was finally able to move and started running toward him, never stopping until she was in his arms. "Oh, James! Oh, James! I was so scared! He was going to set the shed on fire!"

He held her close to him. "Let me take you inside. Then I'll come back out and take a look around."

"He ran into the woods. I scared him. I – I pretended I had a gun. I told him I would shoot!"

"Shh! Just calm down, honey. I'll phone the police. Maybe if they get started right away, they can catch up with him."

She trembled in his arms and stumbled against him as they started walking. Finally, he reached down, took her into his arms and carried her the rest of the way.

She waited on the sofa as he telephoned the police. Then he sat down beside her. "Are you okay?"

She shook her head. "I am now. Oh, James, it's such a beautiful evening. I just meant to walk around in the grass for a minute. Then I heard a sound by the shed, and I hid behind the tree and......"

He kissed her forehead. "It's okay. Try to calm down. I'm here and everything will be okay."

She leaned against him. "Oh, I love you so much! Please, please don't be mad at me about Max and for not telling you about the note! I was so stupid!"

"Never call yourself stupid. You are human." He smiled at her then. "And you are beautiful. And you're mine. And I love you." He kissed her lightly.

"Can you ever forgive me?"

"Honey, I already have."

TWENTY-FOUR

DANI AWOKE THE NEXT MORNING with one thought on her mind. Since Liz was going home today, there would be no more daily visits to the hospital and no more chances of running into Star Light. Even though she'd only seen her there that one time, she held onto the hope that it might happen again.

"You seem distracted," James said over breakfast. "Are you still upset over what happened? Do you need me to stay home with you today?"

The thought was enticing but she shook her head. "No, I'll be fine. In fact, I'm better than fine. I feel so totally blessed and thankful that no disaster happened last night. But right now, I'm thinking about Star."

He grinned. "Star Light. I wonder if that's her real name."

"I wonder if I'll ever see her again."

"She seems strange to me. From everything you've told me, I think it's best if you try to forget about her."

"I can't forget about her. I think I'm supposed to help her."

"But she doesn't want your help. She doesn't want anything to do with you. Remember?"

She sighed. "She's such a beautiful young girl."

"So you've said."

"Why would anyone so pretty be so unhappy?"

"Looks doesn't have anything to do with whether we're happy or sad."

"You're right." She stood up, took both their coffee cups and refilled them. "Will you be working late today?"

"I hope not. What are you doing?"

She didn't tell him about her doctor appointment. The thought of it caused excitement to run throughout her entire body. In just a few short hours, she would know for sure whether or not she was pregnant. She couldn't suppress a smile. "I'll be waiting for you to get home."

He smiled, too. "Now, that's more like it. You have such a beautiful smile." He stood up. "Sorry, honey. I should've told you not to refill my cup. I really have to go." Leaning down, he kissed her lightly. "I love you."

"I love you, too."

The moment the door closed behind him, she looked at the clock. Her appointment wasn't for two more hours. She had her last story finished. What could she do to pass the time?

Once again, she thought of Star. Was she all right? Was her mother still living? Did Star have anyone to help her through the difficult days ahead of her if her mother had passed away?

She had to see her again. For some reason, she knew it for a certainty.

Was it a prompt from God, telling her that Star needed her, whether or not she wanted her, and she would be making a serious mistake if she didn't keep trying to get through to her?

She knew where she lived. If she drove by the trailer court, might she possibly see her there again? If not, she could ask somebody about her, now that she knew her name.

She didn't take time to dwell on it. Instead, she went to her car and started toward the trailer court. Slowing down as she got closer, she wondered if the place looked even more run down than it had before. It saddened her that anyone had to live there. At the same time, she knew there were even worse places and they were all over the world.

She saw children playing. They looked like the same ones she'd seen before and like they were wearing the same clothes. Lord, help them! Driving through the different roads, she searched for someone to talk to. Wasn't anyone out? The other time she was there, there had been several men and women standing around talking. Where was everyone?

Should she go and knock on a door? Parking the car, she started up the walkway toward the closest mobile home and did just that. No one answered and there was no sound from inside to lead her to believe anyone was home. She went to another. Still no answer.

As she started to get into her car again to drive on a little further, one of the children who had been playing came up to her. She couldn't have been more than four or five years old, and was very petite, with long blonde pig-tails and shiny blue eyes. "Who you looking for?" she asked.

Dani smiled, thinking how beautiful she was. "I'm looking for a girl named Star. Do you know her?"

Before she had a chance to answer, a little boy, also blonde with blue eyes, walked over and stood beside her and reached for her hand. Looking at her very seriously, he said, "You know you can't talk to strangers!" Without another word, he pulled the little girl away and they ran off together.

They were so much alike. Could they be twins? It occurred to her that someone loved them enough to instill in them the danger of talking to strangers. With a sigh, she got into her car, drove a short piece further and then stopped again. Surprisingly, the section of the court she was now in was much cleaner, with more modern mobile homes and very well kept.

A small elderly lady with grey hair pulled back in a bun answered the next door that Dani knocked on. When she smiled broadly, her soft blue eyes twinkled behind her wire-rimmed glasses. "Do you need something, honey?"

Dani smiled back. "I'm looking for someone. I think she lives here but I don't know which house is hers."

"And who would she be? I know everybody here."

"Her name is Star. Star Light."

"Oh, yes! I know Star but she isn't home right now, dear. She and her sister took off first thing this morning. She's taking her sister back to……oh, that's of no interest to you, I'm sure. She probably won't be back for a day or so."

Dani couldn't help wondering what the lady had started to say about where Star was taking her sister, but felt it would be rude to ask. "Is their mother at home?"

"Oh, Mrs. Gordon hasn't been feeling well. She just got home from the hospital and she never goes anywhere and she never sees anybody. Just between you and me.......what did you say your name is, honey?"

"Danita, Dani for short. What's wrong with Mrs. Gordon?" At least she finally knew Star's mother's name.

"She has cancer, dear. I like your name. Never heard it before. You named after somebody?"

"No, my mother just liked the name. Is anyone staying with Mrs. Gordon while her daughters are gone?"

"We all look in and check on her when they have to leave. The younger one, well, she makes sure we know we need to do it. Now, Star, she doesn't have a lot to say."

"Star doesn't talk a lot?"

The elderly lady hesitated, then continued. "She more or less just keeps things to herself. Why don't you come on in, honey, and we'll talk awhile? I just made a fresh pot of coffee and we can have a cup."

As Dani followed her inside, her first impression was one of pleasant surprise. Even though the lady's home was very small, it was immaculately clean and smelled of flowers and fresh brewed coffee.

"It isn't much, but it's mine," the lady said with definite pride in her voice. "Come into the kitchen."

"I didn't get your name," Dani said as she sat down by the table. It was covered with a clean red-checkered table cloth and a vase of fresh-cut wildflowers sat in the center.

The lady poured two cups of coffee, set them on the table and sat down across from Dani. "Everybody just calls me

Granny Jane. You can, too, if you want. You don't live around here, do you?"

"As a matter of fact, I do. My house is on the other side of the woods that border this court."

"You don't say. I heard there was a fire in those woods about a week ago, but nobody got hurt. I was glad of that. Do you want some cake, sweetie? You're pretty thin."

"Oh, no, I just had breakfast and I'm not hungry."

"You look a bit peeked around the eyes, now that I see you closer. You okay?"

"I'm fine."

"There's no need to worry about stuff, you know. The good Lord's going to take care of everything."

"Granny Jane, do you know much about Star?"

"She seems to be a good girl, but like I said, she's kind of quiet. Her and her sister both look out for me. That's why I'm sure to look out for their mom when they have to go away."

"Do they go away a lot?"

"No, the sister doesn't live her. Her name is Heaven."

Dani's eyes widened.

Granny Jane snickered. "Sure enough, Dani. I love to watch the expressions on people's faces when I mention those girls' names. One is Star and one is Heaven. Mrs. Gordon sure picked some originals, didn't she?"

"Is Heaven's last name Light, too, or is she a Gordon?"

"Both Star and Heaven are Lights." She chuckled, then continued. "Their father passed away and their mother then married Mr. Gordon, but he's not with them. I don't know where he is. I heard their father was cruel to the girls. A very sad situation. I do hope he changed his ways before he went on to meet his maker."

"What is Mrs. Gordon's first name? Is it unusual, too?"

"Her name is Carol, but most people just call her Mrs. Gordon, for some reason."

Dani took a sip of her coffee. "Oh, this is good! My coffee doesn't taste like this."

Granny Jane grinned. "That's because I have a secret ingredient that I brew with the coffee.   Now, don't ask me what it is because then it wouldn't be a secret any longer, would it?"

Dani laughed. She couldn't help liking this lady. "There are a lot of children here, aren't there?"

"It's hard for young people to buy nice homes now-a-days. A lot of them have to raise their families here, where it's a little cheaper. But those kids are happy and well cared for. Did you see the little blonde twins? Dori and Dana. Sweetest little tykes you ever laid your eyes on."

Dori and Dana.   As Granny Jane continued, Dani pictured again the two children she'd seen a few minutes earlier in her mind.

"You'd think little Dana was two or three years older, the way he watches out for Dori," Granny Jane finally concluded.

They talked awhile longer before Dani looked at her watch and gasped. "Oh, Granny Jane, I have to go. I didn't know it was so late and I have an appointment." She stood up.

Granny Jane stood up as well and walked with Dani to the door. "Do you want me to tell Star you were looking for her?"

"No, I'll try to catch up with her another time. But can you tell me which home she lives in?"

"Two trailers down. It's the blue one with the tan trim and the nice big porch. I'm so glad you came by, Ms. Dani. Will you come back again?"

Dani smiled. "I would love to, and I'd love to take you to my house some time to meet my husband."   She opened the door and stepped outside. "Thank you for the coffee and for the conversation."

"Oh, thank *you*! And, honey….."

Dani looked at her quizzically.

Granny Jane lowered her voice, but her eyes twinkled brighter than ever. "You're going to have a beautiful baby."

TWENTY-FIVE

How HAD GRANNY JANE KNOWN? As she left the doctor's office a little later, Dani was happier than she could remember being in a long time. She was two months pregnant. And she hadn't been sick one single time! She thought of how Liz had been so sick, seemingly for her entire pregnancy. Was Dani just lucky or what? If she hadn't had the other symptoms, she wouldn't have had any idea at all that she was going to have a baby.

She couldn't wait to tell James.

To her dismay, he called to say something unexpected had come up and he was going to be very late. He stressed over and over for her to stay in the house and to be sure and set the security system before she went to bed if he wasn't yet home. After what happened the night before, he was especially concerned for her safety.

The night passed without incident. She had no idea when he came home, but was happy when she opened her eyes the next morning and saw him lying beside her. She could hardly wait for him to wake up so she could tell him the news. Just the same, she got up quietly and tried not to disturb him. He seemed to be sleeping fitfully, which he often did when he was overwhelmed about something or other. It must have been a difficult night for him and there was no telling what time he'd gotten in. She would let him sleep as long as he needed to.

She took a shower, humming the entire time. When she reentered the bedroom, James was sitting up on the edge of the bed.

"You are sure chipper today," he remarked, smiling at her. "Come here and rub some of that joy around on me." He held out his arms.

She went to him and sat down on his lap, then nestled her face against his ear and whispered, "Good morning, Daddy."

He laughed and pulled back slightly. "Daddy? Well, I guess it's never too early to get started seeing what it sounds like, is it? So, good morning back to you, Mommy."

She giggled. She couldn't help it.

"What's so funny? Thinking of a good joke or something?" He kissed her cheek.

"I'm certainly thinking of something good."

"I'm certainly holding something good," he responded, squeezing her a little tighter. "Umm. You smell good, too."

"Mommy's are always supposed to smell good."

Again, he laughed. "Does Daddy smell good? No, don't answer that. I still have my morning breath. I can't smell good."

She brushed her lips against his, then pulled back and scrunched up her nose. "Oh, Daddy smells really bad!"

Before she knew what was happening, he'd playfully pushed her off his lap and onto the floor and jumped to his feet. Then he looked at her, laughed and held out his hands to help her up.

She laughed, too, as she let him pull her to her feet. "I'm not the only one in a good mood."

"I have some exciting news."

She waited.

"I'm only working half a day today. And, oh, we are going to Hawaii!"

Her eyes widened. "Hawaii? Are you saying we're going – *today*?"

"Sorry, it came out wrong. We aren't going today. I made the reservations yesterday. I wanted to surprise you last night but then, as luck would have it, I couldn't get away from the office. So – what do you think?"

She laughed. "I think it sounds wonderful. When are we going? I can't believe you're going to get off work long enough to take such a long trip."

"Well, it's a little while yet til we leave. I was just too excited to wait to tell you. We have plenty of time to wrap anything up that we need to."

She swallowed. "How – long of a little while?" She was already two months pregnant.

"We leave in September."

"September? That – that's six months from now." Nearly time for her to deliver! "If – we need to – could we reschedule?"

"Why would we need to? Honey, I know you've always wanted to go there and....."

"James, in September, I will be just about ready to deliver."

His eyes narrowed. "Deliver? What?"

She laughed. She couldn't help it.

"Dani, what are you talking about?"

"In six more months, I will be eight months pregnant. I don't think I'd enjoy a vacation in Hawaii."

He gasped.

His expression was so surprised and comical that she started to giggle.

James' mouth then formed a large "o". "Oh, my goodness! Are you telling me…? Are you…..? When? How?"

She kept laughing. "Yes, I'm telling you! Yes I am! I'm two months along, and you know how it happened!"

He started to laugh, too, then he picked her up and spun her around in the air. Finally, he let her back down, held her and kissed her. "Oh, honey, I just dumped you onto the floor! What if I'd done something to hurt you? Is it a boy or girl?"

"I don't know yet. I just found out yesterday, when I had my doctor appointment."

"Why didn't you let me go with you?"

"I wanted to surprise you!"

"You sure did that! Oh, my goodness! I'm going to be a father! An honest to goodness father! Who cares anything about going to Hawaii? I'd rather stay right where I am and have a baby!"

OVER BREAKFAST, she told him about her visit to the trailer court. As she expected, he didn't like it that she'd gone back but he soon found himself fascinated with the elderly lady called Granny Jane. He promised that they would go back there together soon so he could meet her.

After her husband left for work, Dani went outside to sit on the porch. She called Liz, simply to see how she was doing since she'd gone home, but they wound up talking over an hour. Sitting quietly afterward, Dani smiled as she remembered how she'd had to hold the phone away from her ear when Liz squealed so loudly after she told her she was pregnant.

Her mind returned to the night before last, when she'd seen the person attempting to burn down their shed. He'd disappeared into the woods and when the police scoured the entire area not long afterward, there was no sign of him. Where could he have gone? The trailer court was directly connected at the other side of the woods. Could it be someone who lived there? Could that be where the nun lived? Why hadn't she thought to ask Granny Jane if there might be a nun there, even if she was just visiting? Or had been visiting three weeks ago, the one and only time Dani had actually seen her. How great was the distance between their wooded property and where it ended at the court? Would it be close enough for a person to travel through by foot? Or could there be a path wide enough for a car?

So many thoughts ran through her mind. As they continued, she found herself leaving the porch and walking through the grass, then stopping at the edge where the wooded area started. After they'd built their home, she and James used to spend a lot of time there, walking, exploring, having picnics. But they hadn't done it for a long time. They were always too busy with their jobs. When they did have time together anymore, they spent it at a restaurant or a movie. Somewhere along the line, the woods had lost their charm.

She thought of the investigation that was conducted after the fire. James had gone in with the team, but she hadn't. Wouldn't he have mentioned it if there'd been a wider than usual path or any evidence of tire tracks?

She walked on, entering the shade of the lush green trees. Remembrance of the last time she'd been there, that day with Max, washed over her and she quickly forced herself to think of something else. Anything – but that.

Surely, it was too far to walk to the trailer court. She thought the woods on their property covered at least an acre. Maybe more. The trailer lot was created on the vacant lot on the other side of the woods later on and had probably been there about 5 or 6 years.

As her mind continued to run on, she kept walking.

To her surprise, it wasn't nearly as far as she'd imagined before she had her first glimpse of the trailer court. A person in fairly good shape could walk, or run, back and forth easily and quickly; perhaps even a nun wearing a long skirt - or an able-bodied man needing a fast getaway when caught in the act of mischief.

She was convinced that whoever was creating so much trouble for her and James was someone who lived in this very court.

TWENTY-SIX

WHEN DANI EMERGED FROM THE WOODS AGAIN, she was surprised to see Max's truck in the driveway. Why was he there? Remembrance of what his mother had just revealed came flooding back to her. She wondered if he was aware that Rita had told her.

When she was half way up the yard, he saw her and got out of the truck. As she watched him walking toward her, tall and slim in his blue jeans and black tee shirt, his blonde hair glistening in the sunlight, she couldn't help thinking how handsome he was - and remembering how he had walked away from her all those years ago with tears in his eyes and lies on his lips.

He smiled as they met in the middle of the yard. "I was just getting ready to leave. I have to admit I was a little concerned when I saw your car in the drive but there was no answer at the door, no matter how loud I banged on it."

"I've been walking."

"Through the woods. Do you often do that?"

"No." She stopped at the porch, turned and looked at him. "Is there some reason you're here?"

"You sound like you're upset with me about something."

She didn't answer, but stepped onto the porch and sat down on the glider. Until then, she didn't realize how far she'd actually walked and she felt tired.

"Have I done something else?"

"Something else?"

He sat down beside her. "Other than kiss you that day? We were getting along so well at the hospital when Liz had her accident, I thought maybe you'd forgiven me, as well as yourself, for kissing me back."

She met his eyes. "I don't ever want to talk about that kiss again. It was a mistake on both our parts and it needs to be forgotten and left out there in the woods or anyplace but in our minds."

"And maybe our hearts?"

"You should probably leave."

"Neighbors might see?"

"I told James everything. He knows there's nothing between us, no matter what somebody might tell him."

"Look, Dani, there's no need for us to get mad at each other, now or ever. I came by, hoping to see both you and James."

"Why would you want to see James?"

"I wanted to tell both of you good bye."

Her eyes widened.

"I'm going back to Florida. I've been talking to my wife, and we've decided to talk about what went wrong between us. Maybe we'll be able to work things out."

"I thought you were already divorced."

"It's not final yet."

"Why did you change your mind?"

He sighed. "Memories. Of you. Of me. I guess I needed to get them out of my system. Maybe that's the real reason I came back here."

She wanted to tell him that she knew the truth about why he'd left her all those years ago, but something inside her wouldn't let her get the words out. Right then, sitting beside him on the swing, he seemed different somehow, more grown-up and mature.

At least she wasn't having any unsettled emotions from his nearness. If it took that one forbidden kiss to get him totally out of her system, she was glad it had happened.

He sighed. "I'll never forget you, Dani, or what we had. But I had no right coming on to you like I did. I messed things up with you a long time ago and then with my marriage. Maybe I thought seeing you again would make everything all right, but all I succeeded in doing was trying to mess up your marriage like I had my own."

She didn't speak.

"I'd like to say I'm sorry for that kiss, but it would be a lie. I may be a heel but I'm not a hypocrite." He stood up. "I need to go. If I stay too long, your neighbors will talk and, whether you want to believe it or not, gossip can cause trouble."

She never moved.

For a moment he stood very still, but then he grinned. "Say, have you seen that nun again?"

She smiled. She couldn't help it. "Do you believe I really saw her? Be honest."

"It sounds far-fetched, but I don't think you've ever lied to me. Why would you lie about that?"

"Nobody else believes me. I'm not even sure James does."

"Have you ever seen her again?"

"No. I'm beginning to think maybe it was my imagination after all."

He laughed.

So did she. Then they laughed together.

He turned serious then. "I hope you have a good life with James, Dani. I mean it."

"I hope you can work things out, too."

"I really think I love her."

"Have you told her?"

"I will."

"Max....

He waited.

"I want you to know that I – that I don't hold anything against you for – what happened between us all those years ago. We were too young. It just wasn't meant to be."

"It was all my fault. I was a fool."

"We're all fools at some time or other. I've done so many things I've regretted in my life. But we can't go back and undo even one of them. All we can do is try to learn from our mistakes and do better in the future."

He didn't answer, but looked down at the ground instead.

She finally said. "I'm glad to know you'll be trying to fix the wrongs in your life and I'll be praying for you and........"

"Sharon."

"For you and Sharon."

"You believe in this prayer stuff?"

"I do."

"So does my mother and dad. They didn't used to have anything to do with it, you know. They've changed. And now that it's happened, my mom is going to die. Doesn't make much sense to me."

"We're all going to die. We just don't know when. You or I, or anyone else, could easily go before Rita does. Death wasn't a sentence that was given only to your mother, Max."

"But it's so doggone scary! I mean, she doesn't even seem to be worried about it, but just the thoughts of it scares me to death."

"But it doesn't have to be scary! Death became the fate of everyone after the initial sin of Adam and Eve. It was a separation from God, the worst thing that could ever happen. But God didn't want to be separated from the creation that He loved. That's why He came up with a plan to give them a chance at redemption. He sent Jesus, His one and only Son, the only person who never committed a single sin, to take all the sins of the entire world on Himself. All we have to do is believe in what Jesus did, and that He died a cruel death on the cross, for our sins, but then He was resurrected. Because He came back to life, so will we. We need only ask for His forgiveness for the sins we've committed and invite him into our hearts. Then we need never fear death, because we know beyond the shadow of a doubt that we will be with the Lord in Paradise, to live again, forever and ever."

"I can't believe all this stuff is coming out of you, Dani. You really and truly believe what you've just said?"

"With all my heart."

He shook his head. "I don't know if I ever can. My mom and dad have both been preaching to me, like you just did. I hate to admit it, but it's one of the things that came between Sharon and me. About a year ago, she started getting all religious, always wanting me to go to church with her, to talk with the preacher. I refused to buy what she was trying to sell."

"No one can sell you salvation. It's a free gift God wants to give everyone on earth. All a person has to do is accept it."

He met her eyes. "But you have to believe it first. It's hard for me to believe anything I can't see with my eyes."

"Do you believe you couldn't live without the air surrounding you? Can you see that air?"

"That's different."

"Is it? Who do you think made that air?"

"It's always been there."

"We don't know that. Was it always here or did it come from the first breath God blew out of His mouth when He created the heavens and earth?"

He sighed. "I never thought I'd hear all this stuff coming from you. I left Sharon to get away from it and here you are, saying the same thing."

She couldn't help smiling. "Do you think it could mean there really is something to it? That it just might be true?"

"Mom and Dad sure seem to believe it. And Sharon."

"Listen to what they're saying, Max. Listen with your heart and mind open. Will you promise me this?"

"I never was much good at keeping my promises to you."

"Then don't make the promise to me. Make it to yourself. Most important of all, make it to God. Give Him a chance to prove Himself to you."

There was a long moment of silence before Max spoke again. "I'll think about it. I'm sure I'll be talking to Sharon about it because she'll see to it that I do. Dani, will you tell Liz good-bye for me? I won't be going by her place again before I leave, but Mom will be keeping me up on her progress, as well as that of the baby." He grinned. "I have to admit, what happened to her was nothing short of a miracle. I was there when they found her. I honestly didn't think she had a chance."

"But God thought differently. It was a miracle. Do you know about the near death experience she had?"

His eyes widened.

Dani smiled. "Why don't you sit back down for a minute and let me tell you a very fascinating, very true story?"

TWENTY-SEVEN

IN CHURCH SUNDAY MORNING, Dani felt as if it were the very first time she'd ever been there. There was such a change in her heart, such a brand new love for the Lord, that she felt happier than she'd ever been in her life. When or where the transition had happened, she wasn't entirely sure. She only knew she'd been doing a lot of praying. Why should she be surprised when God answered?

"I have an idea," James said as they left after the service.

"And that is?"

"Why don't we go get a take-out order at the restaurant, enough for three people, and run by Granny Jane's?"

Dani laughed, delighted. "I think that's a wonderful idea."

So did Granny Jane. She seemed so genuinely happy to see Dani again, as well as to meet James. They spent the entire afternoon there, and when Granny Jane made a pot of coffee, James found out for himself that his wife had not been exaggerating when she'd told him how delicious it was. Just the same, no matter how they both tried, the sweet old lady would not divulge her secret ingredient.

James laughed as he started back to the car a little later. He'd never met anyone who could tell so many interesting stories about the 'good ole days'.

"Oh, I forgot something!" Dani said as she began to open her door. "I'll be right back."

Granny Jane was still standing in the open doorway, watching them and she grinned widely when Dani came back.

"I wanted to ask you something," Dani said. "It may seem like a strange question. Granny Jane, do you know if there is a nun living in this trailer court?"

Granny Jane's eyes narrowed. "A nun?"

"You know, a Catholic sister that...."

Granny Jane laughed. "Oh, honey, I know what a nun is, but as far as I know, there isn't one here. I would've seen her if she was."

Dani believed her. She didn't think there was anything that happened in the court that Granny Jane didn't know about. "Okay, I was just wondering."

"Why would you wonder about something like that, child?"

"Oh...no real reason."

"Don't tell me that. You have a reason."

Dani couldn't help chuckling. "You're right, I do have a reason, but it's kind of a long story. I promise to tell you all about it the next time I come by."

"I won't forget, you know."

"I know. By the way, is Star back home yet?"

"I expect it'll be tomorrow. She's usually gone for two days when she takes Heaven back to college."

So that was where Star was taking her sister. "Thank you, Granny Jane. You take care and I'll see you again soon."

In the car, Dani turned to her husband. "Let's go visit Star's mother."

"Star's mother?"

"Granny Jane told me the first time I was here that she lives in....."

James grinned and interrupted her before she could finish. "I remember. In the blue trailer with the tan trim and the big porch. Mrs. Gordon lives there with her two daughters, Star and Heaven Light."

"The girls are still gone. Star took Heaven back to college. She'll be back tomorrow."

"Why don't we just come back tomorrow? Despite myself, you've got me curious about this Star Light."

"But it might be a good idea to talk to her mother while Star's gone. Maybe I can get some kind of insight as to why Star seems to hate me so much."

"Okay, we'll go see Mrs. Gordon. But don't get your hopes up too high. And be careful what you say. Remember how sick she supposedly is."

"Not supposedly. She really is sick. Granny Jane said so and I don't think she'd lie about it. I just can't see Granny Jane lying about anything."

James laughed. "She is something else, that's for sure."

"She's the kind of granny I'd love to call my own. I only got to know one of mine, you know."

"But she lives in your heart through your mother's stories."

"My other grandma, Dad's mother, isn't a bit like Granny Jane. She always seems so stern and proper."

James laughed again. "Maybe we should bring her to meet Granny Jane. Don't tell her anything about her. Just tell her you want her to meet somebody."

"Now that's a great idea! Maybe some of Granny Jane would rub off on Grandma! Oh, this is the trailer. It has to be."

He stopped the car by the blue trailer with the tan trim and they walked together onto the large porch.

Dani knocked on the door, then knocked again when there was no answer.

They waited. Finally, they heard the shuffling of feet from inside. The door opened just the tiniest bit but they couldn't see who was standing behind it.

"I'm sorry," came a faint voice from within, "but I'm not up to any visitors and I don't want to buy anything you're selling. You may as well go away."

"Mrs. Gordon?" Dani said then. "My name is……"

"It doesn't matter what your name is. Just go away."

The door closed tightly.

Dani looked at James.

"She doesn't want company," James said. "She made it very plain."

"I can see where Star gets her rudeness," Dani answered. "She just slammed the door in our faces."

"She's sick. You have to remember that. When we don't feel well, we do things we wouldn't ordinarily do."

He started the car again. "By the way, what did you ask Granny Jane when you went back there?"

"If there was a nun living in this court."

"You're kidding. You asked her that?"

"You can walk to this trailer court from our house."

"Through the woods? It's at least a mile."

A mile. No wonder she'd been tired when she got back home the day before. She hadn't told James what she'd done. Once she started talking to him about Max's visit and asked her husband to help her pray that Max and his wife would be able to work things out, she never got around to mentioning her trek through the woods.

James spoke again. "Why did you say you can walk there from our house?"

She told him.

He sighed. "Maybe you should get back to writing again. You have an awfully lot of time on your hands to do a lot of crazy things. Why did you want to walk to the trailer court?"

"Don't you see, James? It's close enough that it can be easily walked to! The nun might live there. The person I saw trying to set fire to our shed could live there. They both just disappeared through the woods. Where else could they have gone to?"

"You told me the nun was still there in the woods, hiding somewhere that you couldn't see her, that she told you God wouldn't hear prayers from someone like you. So, she hadn't run to the trailer court."

"But she could've! Later!"

"Nuns live in convents, not trailers."

"Maybe she was there visiting somebody."

"And she was hungry, so she walked a mile to our house to get some of our food."

"Maybe."

"So how did she get into our house? Did she pick the lock or what?"

"Lots of people can pick a lock."

"Granny Jane would've seen her if she was in the trailer court."

"Oh! Just forget it!"

"Okay. But I don't think you will."

TWENTY-EIGHT

No one expected Max to return only three days later. On Wednesday morning, his father woke up to find his mother had passed away in her sleep. Sitting next to her parents and James at the funeral service, Dani's heart went out to him. He had loved his mother deeply and he was so broken. On the front row seat next to him was his father and Max's wife. She was beautiful, Dani couldn't help thinking. Exactly opposite of herself, Sharon had long dark hair and dark eyes. That she cared deeply for Max was clear to anyone who watched as she clung to his arm, brushed tears from his cheeks, and from time to time, gently ran her hands through his hair. Dani was glad she was there for him.

Would his mother's death help to reunite them? She thought of the scripture that said all things worked together for good. She recalled that the verse ended with the words *to them that loved God and are called according to His purpose.* How could it refer to Max, when he'd told her so plainly that he didn't know if he could ever believe? Then again, Rita was a believer. For her son to be reunited with his wife would be what she wanted, wouldn't it? If the scripture could work for one believing person, why couldn't it work through that person to help a non-believer? She liked the sound of that. For some reason, she found herself wondering what Granny Jane might have to say about it.

Dani and James went home after the service and changed their clothes.

"Well, are you ready?" he asked her then.

She smiled. "I am. You're sure you want to go? I'll go by myself if you want me to."

"I want to go. I want to see Star Light once and for all and get everything settled as to why she doesn't like you." Placing his arms around her, he kissed her lightly. "I just can't understand how anyone can not like you."

"You are prejudiced."

He held her close for a moment, nuzzling his face against her hair. "I really felt sorry for Max and his father today. It must be devastating to lose your mother – or your wife."

They stood there, not saying anything more, for a long time before she finally pulled away. "I'm glad Granny Jane called to tell me Star was back."

"Just don't get your hopes up, that because you're standing there at her door, she'll invite you into the house. If she tells us to leave, that's what we'll have to do. I certainly don't want to be escorted home by a policeman."

"Surely she wouldn't go that far."

"How far is that far? Why don't we say a little prayer before we leave?"

"I think that's a wonderful idea. Can I – pray?"

His eyes widened but he smiled broadly. "I'd like that very much."

They bowed their heads and closed their eyes, and she began slowly. "Dear Lord………Lord, You know my heart. You know all things. I don't know why I feel so compelled to help Star, but there must be a reason. Go with us, please – and help us to say and do only what You want us to. My faith and trust are in You, Lord. Amen."

A few minutes later they were stopping the car by the blue trailer with the tan trim. There were lights on inside and the door was open, and they took it as an encouraging sign.

"I have a good feeling about this," she told her husband, smiling at him as they held hands and started up the walkway.

Star met them at the door, not seeming at all surprised to see them.

"Granny Jane said you were coming and I should be nice to you," she said, without the hint of a smile. "Although I have no idea why you're here, I usually do what Granny Jane wants me to." She was dressed in blue jeans, a dark tee shirt and tennis shoes.

Dani couldn't help thinking it was much better than the all black she'd had on the other times she'd seen her.

"I hope you don't mind our being here," Dani said, offering her best smile.

Star didn't smile back. "And if I do?"

"We'll leave, of course," James said.

Star looked at him, as if it was the first time she noticed he was there. For a very long time, her eyes stayed focused on his face, then roved slowly over what seemed to be every inch of him.

Dani began to feel uncomfortable. Why on earth was she staring at him like that? "We were hoping to talk to your mother," she said. "Is she feeling any better?"

Star's eyes never left James. "Why do you want to see my mother?"

Dani could tell James was just as perplexed as she was by Star's unwavering attention to him, as well as her directing her question to him and not his wife.

"Granny Jane told us she was sick," James answered quickly. "We were wondering if there was anything we could do to help."

"How come you know Granny Jane anyway?" Still to James.

He smiled, hoping to shake his uneasiness. "I kind of thought everyone did."

Star finally turned toward Dani. "Look, I think it would be much better if you two just went back home."

A voice from inside called out weakly. "Star! Who's out there with you, honey?"

Star opened the screen door and answered. "It's just a couple of strangers. They're trying to find somebody."

"Who?"

"Nobody who lives in this court." Star closed the door again and looked back at Dani, then at James. "You'd better leave now. I don't want her coming out here to see if she can help you find somebody. She's weak."

"But…" Dani began.

"It's okay," James interrupted. "We'll go." As he started the car, he said softly, "She reminds me of somebody I used to know."

"Who?"

"A friend."

They stopped at Granny Jane's.

"Star wouldn't let you in," Granny Jane said as soon as they were sitting around her kitchen table.

"Is something wrong with her?" Dani asked. "She was scrutinizing James like he was some kind of villain and she was trying to memorize his face to identify him! The first time I saw her, she was staring at me for no reason, and scowling. Any time I saw her after that, when I tried to start a conversation, she wouldn't talk to me. I can't understand why she doesn't like me when she doesn't even know me. And why on earth did she look at James like she did? I want to just walk away and forget all about her, but at the same time, I have this insatiable feeling that she's needing me to help her. I'm so confused. Why does God keep sending me back to her, only to have her push me away every time?"

Granny Jane smiled. "For ye have need of patience, that, after ye have done the will of God, ye might receive the promise. That's in Hebrews."

"So you're saying I shouldn't give up on her?"

"Only if the Lord tells you to."

"How will I know?"

"You will know."

James looked at his wife, then at Granny Jane and a smile crossed his lips. "You know what would make me feel better than anything right now? A cup of that mysterious coffee that Granny Jane makes."

Granny Jane smiled, then laughed and Dani did the same. At least temporarily, the tension and stress were all gone.

TWENTY-NINE

DANI PULLED AND TUGGED. She held her breath and then yanked really hard. Finally! The zipper was up. She whirled around in front of her mirror. She didn't think she looked any bigger but her stomach was definitely growing. Her favorite jeans had never been so tight. When the time came for her to use the rest room, would she even be able to fasten them again?

There was only one thing to do. She had to go shopping. She didn't yet need maternity clothes but she needed something that had a little stretch in it, an elastic waist instead of a zipper and snap closing. She smiled at the thought, remembering how she had teased Liz when she'd started wearing elastic-waist pants when Liz was pregnant with Tommy.

If only Liz was able to go shopping with her, they would have such a great time. Just like they used to. Her best friend was healing, but she still needed a lot more time before she would be up to a shopping spree. By then, the baby would be big enough to leave the hospital and she'd be too busy. Dani smiled. It was all worth it to have a baby. She was so excited about her own, and she'd never seen James so happy. He would be such a good father.

She finally decided that standing there thinking wasn't going to get her a new pair of jeans, grabbed her keys and headed to her favorite department store.

She couldn't believe it when the first person she saw when she came out of the dressing room after trying on a stack of clothes was Granny Jane. Running over to her, she gave her a big hug.

"Well, Dani, hello!" A wide smile crossed the lips of the sweet old lady.

"How did you get here, Granny Jane?"

"Star brought me. She told me to stay as long as I want, to just call her when I'm ready and she'll come back for me."

"That was sweet of her."

"There's sweetness in everyone if we just look for it."

"You won't have to call her to come back for you, though. I'll take you home when you're ready to go. What are you looking for?"

"I need a new church dress. Maybe you can help me find one."

Dani laughed. "I'll not only find you the prettiest dress in the store, I'll buy it for you. Now, let me pay for the things I have in my cart and the rest of the day is yours."

"I don't need all day to buy a dress."

"You've never shopped with me before." Dani winked. "Do you know what kind of dress you want?"

"Well, I don't want any low necks or high skirts to make those old men out there that have nothing to do but lolly-gag around start making google eyes at me."

Dani had to turn around to keep Granny Jane from seeing her laugh. "What size do you wear?"

"I'll have to check the tag in this dress I have on. It's been a while since I bought a dress."

Dani looked at her again, then peeked at the tag. "This is a size 14, but it's pretty big on you. I think you need about a 10."

"This one is a little too big. It fit when I bought it about ten years ago."

"Ten years ago?"

"When I get something I like, I hold onto it. But I was bigger then. In fact, I was really getting pudgy so I went on a diet. When I lost weight, I just pulled the belt tighter, like it is now. But you know what, honey? I thought I'd be much happier and more content if I lost the weight, but it didn't make a bit of difference. I was happy either way, fat or skinny. It's just what's inside a person, not what they look like on the outside. I just decided to stay skinny so I'd be healthy, but no other reason."

"That makes perfect sense."

They had lunch at McDonald's, despite Dani's plea to treat Granny Jane to a good meal at one of her favorite restaurants. She didn't need any of that fancy food, the old lady told her. She loved hamburgers. She ate so many vegetables and so much food that was good for her at home that she wanted something sinfully delicious when she went out. Like a Big Mac! Dani teased her, telling her there was no way she could eat all of it. Granny Jane surprised her by finishing every bite and topping it off with an apple pie.

"I could just about eat an ice cream cone," Granny Jane then said.

Dani laughed. "Not me. I'm too full."

"Okay, we'll have one later. Let's go buy that dress now so we can have some fun. I want that first one I tried one, the blue one. Didn't it make the blue in my eyes really stand out?"

"It sure did."

"You know what I'd really like to do since I'm done shopping?" Granny Jane asked her as they were leaving the store. "And, thank you for paying for the dress for me, and for the shoes."

"What would you like to do?"

"Go to the park. I used to love the park but I haven't been there in a long time. It's still here, isn't it?"

"It sure is."

Granny Jane stopped suddenly. "Just a minute, honey."

Dani was surprised when the old lady grabbed the arm of a young black boy walking toward the door. He was dressed in the youthful style of the day – baggy pants, big shirt, and big curly hair. What was she doing?

"Young man?" Granny Jane said to him.

He looked at her, with neither a smile nor frown. "Yea? You talkin' to me?"

"I sure am. Son, this young lady here just bought me a new dress and a new pair of shoes and I just met her. What she did made me so happy. You got a mama?"

"Yea, I got a mama."

Dani could hear the snickering behind his words but it didn't seem to faze Granny Jane in the least.

"How long's it been since you bought her something?" Granny Jane then asked him. As she talked, she was rooting through her large purse.

The boy said nothing, but just stood there shaking his head as if he thought the old lady was crazy.

She held out her hand. "Here's some money. You get something for your mama. Even if it doesn't really make her happy, it will make you happy."

His eyes wide, the boy took the money and started walking again.

Granny Jane called after him. "Remember, son, God sees everything you do. He's gonna know for sure what you really do with that money and it's gonna go in the record book in heaven."

Dani snickered as they walked on. She'd never in her life met anyone like this woman!

When Granny Jane didn't say much as they leisurely strolled through the park a short time later, Dani imagined she had to be getting tired and would be wanting to go home soon.

But there was no end to Granny Jane's surprises. "Now, Dani, honey," she said after a while, "if I wear you out, you just sit down on a swing or something and rest. Okay?"

If she wore her out. Dani smiled, then laughed aloud.

Granny Jane looked at her. "Well, you are having a baby, you know."

"How old are you, Granny Jane?"

Granny Jane grinned. "I'll be 93 on my next birthday. God sure has been through a lot with me in all these years."

She just bet He had!

"You know what I liked the best of anything at the park when I was young?"

"I'd say you liked everything about it," Dani replied.

"See that big ole sliding board. I loved it! I was up and down that ladder, sliding down over and over and over. I'd go on my seat, on my belly, head first or feet first. Boy, was it fun." As she talked she was walking over to it and looking at it wistfully. "You know, I'd love to take just one more ride."

Dani's eyes widened. "You want to go down the slide?"

"I sure do."

"But, Granny Jane……"

"You think I'm too old?"

"No, it isn't that. You have a dress on."

Granny Jane laughed and opened her purse, then started rooting around in it.

"What are you looking for?"

She pulled out her hand, holding tightly to two large safety pins, looked at Dani and grinned. "I always try to be prepared for anything. Would you help me pull this skirt around my legs and pin it together?"

Trying her best to keep a straight face, Dani did as she asked. Then she watched as the old lady began to climb the ladder slowly, one step at a time. Dani held her breath after each one, scared to death she would fall.

At the top, Granny Jane looked down on her. "Gee, it feels good to be up here. Look how much closer to God I am!"

'Don't get too close that He keeps you', Dani thought but she merely said, "Be careful."

Granny Jane laughed so loudly Dani was sure she could be heard all through the park as she carefully seated herself and then let herself go.

Neither of them had been aware of the other children nearby. Dani was surprised when she heard clapping and shouting. Then she saw a small boy running toward the bottom of the slide and standing there with his arms stretched out, waiting to catch the old lady when she stopped.

"Way to go!" he said, grasping her hands and holding her steady against his little body. "I'm gonna do this when I'm old like you. I'm never gonna stop having fun, just like you!"

"You gonna go again, Granny?" asked a smaller girl.

Granny Jane laughed and hugged the little boy. "Thank you, young man. You're a real gentleman. Remember, God sees everything you do and He sure is smiling at you right now!

If it hadn't been for you, I would've sailed right off the end. That slide sure is slick!" She then hugged the girl. "Not this time, honey, but it sure was fun."

Dani stood watching, shaking her head in amazement. Was there anything Granny Jane wouldn't do? She felt a bit like the little boy and hoped she could never stop having fun either!

"I used to drive," Granny Jane told her when they started home. "I was a wild one on the road in my day."

"I'll bet you were."

"You know, I can still drive. Just because I got so old doesn't mean I don't remember everything I ever knew."

"You still have your license?"

Granny Jane laughed. "Heavens no! But I can drive." She sighed. "What I wouldn't give to get behind that wheel, just one more time."

Dani tried to ignore the urge that ran through her as she listened to the wistfulness in Granny Jane's voice. What would it hurt to pull over and just let her sit behind the wheel? She didn't have to actually let her drive.

"I beat some big old boys in a race one time," the old lady went on. "Boy, were they mad! But I made them a batch of cookies and they got over it."

"How old were you then?"

"Thirteen."

Dani gulped.

Granny Jane laughed.

They rode on.

"This is sure a nice car," Granny Jane said after a while. "Bet it's a lot easier to drive than the old clunkers I used to have."

Dani looked over at her for a moment. "You know I can't let you drive, but if you'd just like to sit behind the wheel and reminisce, I'll pull over and let you."

Granny Jane's eyes widened with eager excitement.

Laughing, Dani pulled off the highway and exchanged places with the old woman.

"Oh, just look at all these gadgets!" Granny Jane touched everything on the dashboard that was within her reach. "And there's no clutch to wear your legs out and no gears to keep shifting. Up and down. Up and down. I remember when Harry, that's my late husband, bought our first automatic shift car. It was like going out of a nightmare and into a dream."

Dani smiled, thinking that the more she was with this lady, the more she loved her. Listening as Granny Jane talked on, she turned her eyes to look out the window. It was such a beautiful day and she'd enjoyed every single minute of it. As her mind reverted to the weather, she wasn't aware of what the lady beside her was actually saying or doing. Until the car suddenly started moving.

"Granny Jane!"

The old lady laughed as she peeled out onto the highway. "I still got it, Dani!"

"Oh, no! You have to pull back over and stop. You don't have a license, remember?"

Granny Jane kept going, moving her hands around expertly on the steering wheel. "I'm good. See, I know what I'm doing. It's okay, honey."

"But....."

Granny Jane went faster.

"You really need to slow down."

"This is so much fun! I feel like I'm thirteen again! Wonder what ever happened to those boys."

What was going to happen to *them*?

Granny Jane glanced briefly into the rearview mirror just then. "Oughto!"

"Oughto?" No sooner was the word out of her mouth than Dani caught her first glimpse of a flashing red light directly behind the car.

Granny Jane slowed down and expertly pulled over, stopping the car.

Dani's heart was racing. What would happen now? What would they do to Granny Jane for not only driving but also speeding without having a license? What would they do to *her*?

Granny Jane looked at her and grinned. "Don't worry, honey. God's got this."

Dani sighed, wishing she had even half of Granny Jane's faith at the moment.

Granny Jane rolled down the window and smiled at the young policeman that was standing there.

A look of surprise entered his eyes when he saw her and a large grin crossed his lips. "Granny Jane! What in the world are you doing driving?"

"Well, Johnny Carter! I haven't seen you in forever, since you were knee high to a grasshopper! You look just the same, though. How is your mama?"

"Mama's doing great. Now Granny Jane, about your driving……"

"I was good, wasn't I? Did I surprise you?"

"You surprised me all right." He turned his eyes toward Dani, who was watching and listening. "And who might you be, Mam? Could I see your license and registration?"

Dani had already pulled them out and handed them to him. He seemed nice enough, but he had a duty to perform and she didn't think it would be letting Granny Jane get away with her little fiasco.

He looked at the cards, then back at Dani. "Danita Starrman? Do you know James Starrman?"

Granny Jane chuckled and answered for Dani. "She not only knows him, she's married to him, and they're going to have a baby."

The patrolman smiled even wider. "Well, what about that? Mrs. Starrman, I interviewed with your husband the other day for a technician position. He called me just yesterday and said I was hired! This is my last day on this job that I absolutely hate." He handed her back her cards. "What do you say we just let you get back under that wheel and pretend this little incident never happened? I mean, Granny Jane didn't hurt anybody. Granny Jane wouldn't hurt a flea if it was biting the life out of her!"

"And this is your last day," Granny Jane reminded him, unbuckling her seat belt.

He laughed. "And this is my last day!" Leaning in the window he kissed the top of the old lady's head. "I love you, Granny Jane, but don't you dare try to drive again. Do you hear me?"

"Loud and clear."

Dani shook her head in disbelief as she started down the highway again.   "You told me the Lord would take care of everything," she said. "Why am I always so surprised when He does exactly the right thing, every single time?"

"I got a little problem, Dani."

Her lightheartedness quickly changed to fear as she looked over at the old lady, who was hunched over in the seat and holding her hands across her stomach. "Are you okay?"

"Too much excitement, I think. Now, I gotta pee. Really bad."

Relief surged through Dani. She simply needed to use the rest room. Seeing a gas station just ahead, she pulled in and stopped.

"I'll just be a minute," Granny Jane told her as she went inside.

Dani sat there, smiling as she recalled everything that had happened that day. She hadn't had so much fun in a long time. Granny Jane might be old, but she was as spry as someone half her age and she laughed and joked so much she kept Dani continually laughing. And the things she did! She thought of the boy she'd given the money to. She doubted that he'd spend it on his mother, but she didn't think he'd forget what Granny Jane told him either.

She could still see Granny Jane on the top of that sliding board, her dress pinned between her legs, getting ready to sail down, and the little boy at the bottom, waiting to catch her. A fit of giggles overcame her. She couldn't stop them.

She jumped in surprise and her laughter stopped abruptly when someone tapped on her window. Seeing a young man standing there, trying to get her attention, she rolled down her window, smiled and asked him if he needed something.

Her smile froze when he replied. "I sure do. I need this car and I'll take you as a bonus." He was opening the door before she realized what was happening. "Just slide over quietly and I promise not to hurt you."

Shock and terror ran through her entire body. He was going to take her car and kidnap her! The parking lot was empty and there was no one around to stop him. What could she do?

He was starting to give her a push when a loud, stern voice stopped him. "I wouldn't do that if I were you, young man."

Granny Jane! Oh, God. She had no idea that this man might be a murderer! Lord, please help!

The man turned around and laughed. "And I suppose you are going to stop me, old woman?" Looking back at Dani, he started shoving her again.

Only Dani could see Granny Jane reaching into her purse. "No, but this might." She pulled out a small pistol and clicked it. "Now, get away from that car."

The young man's laughter died as he caught sight of the gun. "You wouldn't have the nerve to use that thing. You probably don't even know how," he sneered.

"Maybe I do and maybe I don't but there's no doubt that God does. Now move!" Her voice was threatening.

A siren caught everyone's attention, as well as the patrol car peeling into the station. The would be robber started running, but didn't get far before he was apprehended by none other than the same Johnny Carter that had stopped them just minutes earlier.

"Are you all right, Granny Jane? Mrs. Starrman?"

"We're fine," Dani replied, her voice quivering as she spoke.

Granny Jane looked at the unsmiling young man who was now handcuffed. "God sent this young officer to save you from being shot, young man. You better think about this and change your ways or He might not let you get out alive the next time. You sure better thank the Lord that you're going to jail right now and not the funeral home."

On the road again, Dani sighed deeply.

"You okay?" Granny Jane asked her.

"Is there anything you don't have in that purse of yours? I would never have dreamed you had a gun!"

Granny Jane laughed and pulled out her pistol, waving it front of Dani's eyes. "It sure looks real, don't it?"

Dani gasped. "It's a toy! You took on a man who might be a dangerous criminal – with a toy gun!"

"No. I did it with a real God."

THIRTY

DANI KNEW SHE'D NEVER FORGET the day she spent with Granny Jane. As she told her husband about it and they laughed together, she knew she wanted to do it again. When Sunday came, she invited the old lady to church with them and Granny Jane accepted right away. Of course, there was no way anything unusual would happen in church, Dani told herself as they entered the building. It was just nice to have Granny Jane there with them.

The singing had just started. Although no one else in the ordinarily quiet church had ever done so, Granny Jane started clapping her hands. Heads turned to look and Dani merely smiled at them, thinking that maybe they ought to do some clapping, too. Following Granny's lead, she put her hands together. James looked at her, first with surprise and then with a smile, and then started clapping himself. Before long others joined in. Someone shouted "amen" while another shouted "hallelujah". The singing became more spirited as the ones in the choir started clapping, too. The congregation stood up and joined in the singing.

"Praise God!" Granny Jane shouted, thrusting her hands into the air.

"Amen, sister!" called someone from the back of the church.

It went on for seemingly a long time before the choir stopped and the minister walked up front to the podium. Never had he preached like he did that morning. He was more enthusiastic than he'd ever been and his message was strong and powerful. Before the service ended, several in the congregation had gone to kneel at the altar to pray and make professions of faith, including Dani, James and Granny Jane.

Dani felt light as a feather as she left the church. "Wow!" she said as they got into the car again.

Granny Jane laughed. "You can say that again, honey! God is certainly a wow kind of fellow! I love this church. Can I come with you again some time?"

James smiled. "You can come all the time!" His own heart had been deeply touched and enlightened. All because one little old woman had started to clap her hands!

"Funny," Granny Jane responded, "but that's the same thing your preacher told me when he shook my hand at the door."

Granny Jane called Dani often after that and she wasn't surprised when the phone rang early Tuesday morning and she saw her name on the caller ID. James had just left for work and it was the perfect time to talk.

She needed a favor. It seemed that Star's mother was back in the hospital. Would it be a great inconvenience for Dani to take her to see her? She usually had any number of people to take her where she needed to go, Granny Jane told her, but for some reason she couldn't get any one of them today. Dani didn't hesitate for a moment. Not only could she be with Granny Jane again, it was another opportunity to try to help Star.

As she had done before, Granny Jane talked during the entire drive. She commented on the weather, saying how beautiful it was, even though it was rainy and dismal. Then she remarked on how her legs had been hurting when she got up that morning but how thankful she was to have legs to hurt. She mentioned her grandson that she hadn't seen for several years, saying that she 'felt it in her bones' that he would be coming to visit her very soon and she was excitedly waiting for him.

Dani merely listened, never losing a smile, as she kept thinking what a different world it would be if everyone was more like the elderly lady sitting beside her in the car.

She was surprised when the two of them entered the hospital room and she had her first look at Mrs. Gordon. Dani had imagined her being older, since she was so sick, as well as the fact that everyone called her Mrs. Gordon, but she didn't look to be over forty at the most. She was beautiful. She had the same dark hair and eyes as Star, but she was very slim. Of course, sickness could've caused weight loss.

"This is Danita, Mrs. Gordon, Dani for short," Granny introduced her as she sat down in a chair near the bed. "Dani was kind enough to drive me here. We just met recently but I feel like she's always been my friend. She's almost like the daughter I never had, to be truthful, or granddaughter." She chuckled.

Mrs. Gordon, sitting up in bed, looked at Dani and smiled.

What a lovely smile! "I'm really happy to meet you, Mrs. Gordon," Dani said.

"My name is Carol. I sort of wish people would start calling me that, instead of Mrs. Gordon."

Granny Jane's eyes narrowed. "I didn't know you wanted to be called by your given name, Mrs. – Carol. Why didn't you say something before?"

Carol laughed and the sound was delightful. She didn't seem, to Dani, to be so terribly sick. "Its okay, Granny Jane. *You* can call me anything you want to."

Dani sat down in the other bedside chair. "I figured Star would be here."

"You know Star?"

"We've met."

"I'm sure she'll be here soon. It was pretty late when she brought me in last night and she's probably tired. Maybe even still in bed. I told her I didn't need to come but she insisted. My girls are so protective of me."

Granny Jane spoke. "I guess that's why she didn't answer when I called to ask her if she'd bring me. How long will you have to stay this time?"

"The doctor hasn't been in yet this morning but I'm sure I'll get to go back home when he does. Because of my condition, they usually keep me overnight just to check me out. I have cancer," Carol said, directly to Dani. "It was supposed to have killed me a couple years ago, but I'm still here for some reason. The only thing it killed was my hair." She lifted her beautiful dark hair, which turned out to be a wig, from her head and then replaced it. "I miss my hair."

Dani's heart went out to her. She was sick and supposedly dying and her only real concern was her hair.

"The Lord can heal you, you know," Granny Jane said.

"I know He can. For Star's sake, I pray daily that He will."

Why did she mention only Star? What about her other daughter?

Carol seemed to know exactly what Dani was thinking. "Heaven, even though she's younger than Star, is already much more secure in her life and I have no doubt she can take care of herself, no matter what happens. Star……well, since you've met her, you've probably noticed that she's kind of withdrawn. She worries about everything, especially me. She can't keep a job because she's always taking days off to be with me, even though I tell her I'm okay. I don't think she has any friends, like Heaven does. She's too busy dwelling on the past – she has been through a great deal, but so has Heaven – to look for a brighter tomorrow."

"I've tried to talk to her," Dani said, "but she doesn't like me for some reason. I don't know why and it puzzles me. I have to be honest with you, Carol, it bothers me." She smiled then. "Maybe she needs to spend more time with Granny Jane."

Granny Jane laughed. "Now, honey, I'm just an old woman. How could I help little Star?"

Carol spoke. "I agree with Dani, Granny Jane. You've uplifted me more times than I can count, but Dani, Star's problem is deep rooted. She never knew her real father and her step father mistreated her. But he was no kinder to Heaven, who was his own flesh and blood. I can't understand why one child can get over a bad situation and move on and another can't."

"Has she seen a counsellor?"

"After Joe passed, her stepfather, I took her to a couple different ones, but it only seemed to make things worse. I guess we never found the right person for her particular problem."

"What about a minister?"

"She wants nothing to do with church or anything pertaining to it. She always argues that her real father that she never knew was supposedly a Christian and he still abandoned her. I've tried to explain the circumstances to her, but, well, I could never get through to her." Carol stopped, took a deep breath and then went on. "I don't know why I'm telling you all this, Dani. I don't even know you."

"I'd like to be your friend. If there's anything I can do for either you or Star, I'd like to be here for you. I can't help wondering about Mr. Gordon."

"At first, Jerry Gordon was good to me and to the girls, but then he turned out to be no better than Joe, Mr. Light, because when I got sick, he left. At least Joe had a choice. He died. Jerry simply didn't want burdened with a sick wife who could no longer take care of two daughters that weren't even his. That's when the girls and me moved back here and into the trailer court. You see, I was raised here in North Carolina but we moved to New York when I was a teen ager. But with my parents gone – they died in an accident when I was twenty-five – and no longer having a husband, I couldn't afford to stay there. So I came back here. We've been here for nearly a year now."

They were interrupted by the appearance of the doctor. He checked Carol's vitals, talked for a few moments, went over her chart, and told her she could go home.

"That was short and sweet," Carol commented when he was gone. "But then again, he knows my case so well that he'd know immediately if there was any new problems. Granny Jane, would you hand me my purse from that little drawer over there? I'll call Star and have her come get me."

"But I can drive you home," Dani said immediately.

"That's really sweet of you, Dani, but I don't want to be a bother."

"It's no bother. I live not far from you and it won't even be out of my way."

"Are you sure?"

"She's sure," Granny Jane said. "Now let us help you get dressed and we'll be on our way."

Star was sitting on the porch when Dani pulled into the driveway. Her eyes widened when she saw her mother in Dani's car. Jumping up immediately, she ran over and started to help Carol out.

"I'm fine, Star, really," Carol said. "I think you've met Dani. She was kind enough to drive me home."

"Why are you home so soon? Don't they care anything about you at that hospital? How do they know you're well enough to be let out already?" One question after the other fell from Star's lips.

Dani watched her. That she loved her mother and was very concerned for her health was clearly apparent within her voice and her actions. As Star led her mother up the walkway, then insisted she be seated on the porch swing she had just vacated, Dani and Granny Jane followed

Star looked up then, meeting Dani's gaze. "She's okay now. I'll take care of you. You don't have to stay."

Granny Jane spoke. "We'd really like to stay for a while, if it's okay, Star."

"Of course you can stay," said Carol before her daughter could answer. "Sit down. Star, please get us each a glass of water. I don't know about them, but I'm terribly thirsty."

Star disappeared into the house, but not before she glanced at Dani and Dani saw the look of disdain in the younger girl's eyes.

Why didn't she like her? All Dani had done from the first time she'd seen Star was try to be nice to her. She'd smiled at her. She'd tried to talk to her. Over and over, she'd asked her if there was any way she could help her. Dani couldn't count the number of prayers she'd said on her behalf. Nothing was working, not even the pleas to God. Why?

Upon impulse, Dani said, "I'll help Star. It will be hard for her to carry all those glasses by herself."

She followed Star to the kitchen and waited until the girl turned around and saw her. Then she said, "Why don't you like me? What have I done? Tell me, and I'll stop doing it."

Star smirked. "You really have no idea, have you?"

"No, I don't."

Reaching into the refrigerator, Star pulled out a pitcher of water and started pouring it into glasses. She didn't say anything else until all of them were filled. Then she met Dani's gaze. "Maybe if I tell you, you'll go away and never come back. Just like he did."

Dani waited, having no idea what she meant.

"I never thought it would be so easy to find you when I moved here, but I was surprised to find out you were close enough to walk to. What luck, huh?"

"Why were you looking for us?"

Ignoring the question, Star continued. "You know, I thought of being a nun once."

Dani felt her heartbeat involuntarily quicken as the memory of the nun she'd thought she'd seen flashed through her mind. Why had Star said that?

"I still have the habit that I was supposed to wear. I keep it hidden in the woods and sometimes I put it on and pretend that God loves me when I'm wearing it."

"God does love you, Star."

Star laughed and continued as if Dani hadn't spoken. "I had it on that first time I went to your house. You saw me in it that day. That was me. It was so easy to get into your house, and you had so much food. I was entitled to every single thing I took."

"If I'd known you needed food, I would've given it to you," Dani said softly, unable to believe what she was hearing. She really *had* seen a nun running that day. It wasn't her imagination. It had been Star!

"I set the fire in the woods, too."

"Why?" Dani breathed.

"Because I hate you."

Dani swallowed. From the seething within her voice, there wasn't a doubt in her mind that Star was telling the truth. For some reason, she truly hated her.

"I would've burned down that shed if you hadn't stopped me. Did you really have a gun? Would you have shot me in cold blood? I couldn't take the chance."

Dani's heart raced even faster.

Star went on. "I saw you – and that blonde haired guy. I was right there behind a tree where I could see it all. How you melted in his arms! I even heard your moans of pleasure. It was the first and only time I felt sorry for *him.*"

"Him?" Why had she felt sorry for Max?

"Your husband. James Starrman."

"You know James?"

"Oh, no. He made sure of that."

"What do you mean?" Dani was becoming more and more confused.

"I mean, *Danita,* that I never had a chance to know him because he deserted me when I was a baby! James Starrman, your husband, the man I was actually named after, is my biological father!"

All the blood seemed to drain from her body as Dani stared at Star. She was lying! She had to be. She was making everything up from pure spite. Why?

As Star stood perfectly still, staring at her, Dani turned and fled from the room. As she ran back onto the porch, then down the steps and toward her car, her heart felt as if it was going to jump out of her chest and all of a sudden it was hard for her to breathe.

"Dani!" Granny Jane called after her.

"Dani? Is something wrong?" Carol wanted to know.

She didn't answer. She simply got into the car, started the engine and drove away.

She had to talk to James. *Immediately*!

THIRTY-ONE

JAMES WAS SITTING ON THE PORCH when she peeled into the driveway a few minutes later. It surprised him that she'd come in so recklessly, then again when she jumped out of the car and just stood there, staring at him.

Was something wrong? Why was she looking at him like that? He went to meet her and started to put his arm around her, but she pulled away immediately. When she looked up at him, he noticed that her eyes were filled with tears. "Dani?"

She started to say something but no words came from her lips. All she could do was stand there, looking at him and crying.

James was quickly becoming not only concerned, but also frightened. "Are you all right? Has something happened?" Again, he tried to put his arm around her but again she resisted.

"Dani? Honey, what is it?"

She said only one word. "No!" Then she grimaced, raised her hand across her chest and started to fall.

His eyes wide with terror, he caught her before she hit the ground. "Dani! Dani!"

She didn't move. She just lay there in his arms, seemingly lifeless.

"Oh, my God! What on earth is wrong?" Panic-stricken, James wondered what to do. Should he call an ambulance? Should he take her to the hospital himself?

She stirred then and opened her eyes. For a moment, she simply stared at him. Then she asked him what had happened and why he was standing there in the driveway holding her like that.

Before he had a chance to answer, she sighed deeply, and told him she remembered everything and she had to talk to him about it.

He didn't put her down, but instead carried her onto the porch and set her on the glider. Then he sat down beside her. When she didn't say anything right away, he didn't try to prompt her. She would tell him when she was ready and he didn't want to upset her again prematurely. For a few moments, they swung back and forth slowly in silence. To his relief, she seemed to becoming calmer and when he looked at her, she even offered him the glimpse of a smile.

When Dani realized she was feeling much better, she wondered if someone was saying some special prayers for her. It had to be James. Or Granny Jane. Granny Jane had known how upset she was when she ran from the house. So had Carol. Maybe they'd sent up some prayers, too.

"I'm sorry I gave you such a scare, James. I had no idea my body would ever react that way. I thought I was stronger than that. It just goes to prove that none of us is any stronger than our weakest point."

"What was it that triggered your weakest point?"

"Star."

"Star?"

She looked directly into his eyes. "She told me she did all those things that have been happening. She stole the food. She was dressed as a nun one time. She set the fire in the woods and tried to burn the shed."

"Star did that? But why? Did she tell you why?"

"Yes."

He waited.

"She hates us."

"That isn't much of an answer. Why would she hate us when she doesn't even know us?"

"She knows you."

"Me? I only saw her one time, that day we stopped to visit and she wouldn't let us go in."

"You said something that day. You said she reminded you of someone you used to know. Who did she remind you of, James?"

"What does that have to do with anything? You aren't making sense."

"James." She paused, looking at the porch floor and then looking into the yard before turning to him again. "James....."

He waited.

"Star told me that her biological father abandoned her at birth. She told me that --- you are him."

His eyes widened and so did his mouth. "She told you that I'm her father? She's lying! I promise you on a stack of Bibles that I never had a child and abandoned it!"

She looked at him closely for a long moment, then smiled as relief surged through her. "Oh, I knew it had to be a lie! I knew you could never do something like that."

"Are you sure you believed that? Or did a part of you wonder if she could be telling the truth? You were a total wreck when you got here. You even fainted."

She didn't answer him because she was ashamed to admit even to herself that she had believed Star. Even if just for a moment, she really had believed her.

James spoke again. "I want you to tell me everything that happened today. What led up to the things that girl said to you?"

"First of all, Granny Jane called. She said Mrs. Gordon, Star's mother, was back in the hospital and she wondered if I'd take her over to see her. I did. Then Carol was released and I drove her back home."

"Carol?"

"That's Mrs. Gordon's first name. Anyway, Star was there and Carol asked her to get us all some water. I went inside and asked Star, straight out, why she didn't like me." She continued, repeating everything Star said after that.

"And Star even told you my name?"

"Not only that, she said that she's named after you."

"Star. Starrman. You said her mother's name is Carol?" James eyes widened suddenly and he gasped. "Oh, my God! No! It can't be!"

"What?"

He swallowed, feeling as if his heart was one big lump that was going to choke him if he didn't. It couldn't be. There was no way.

"Tell me! You're scaring me by just sitting there."

"I've got to start at the beginning. You can't interrupt me until I'm finished."

She waited for him to continue.

"There's something I never told you."

"What are you trying to say?"

"I'm saying that….. Dani, when I was not quite 18, I met a girl named Carol and I fell for her, hook, line and sinker. We started going out and were certain we were in love. She was beautiful, funny, and so much fun to be with." He paused a moment, as if trying to collect his thoughts. "We slipped off once, planning to run away and elope, but her parents found out and stopped us. It only made our desire for each other deepen. And then…….." He swallowed. "She told me she was pregnant."

Dani gasped, but his eyes stopped her from speaking.

"We were happy about it because we were sure her parents would have to let us get married. But, instead, they insisted she have an abortion. She was too young. She was only 17, and had her whole life ahead of her. They forbid us to see each other. They took her for the abortion – and then they moved away – and I never saw her again."

She couldn't believe what he was telling her. Not that she had any doubt that he'd loved someone else before he loved her, but the fact that he'd fathered a child with her. In the entire ten years of their marriage, he'd never said a word about it.

"I guess you're wondering why I never told you. Maybe for the same reason you never told me about Max. I'd never been hurt so badly in my life as when they killed my child and then took Carol away from me. I was so sure she'd write or call, that someday we'd be together again. But there was never a word. Nothing. She was gone from my life forever. I thought I would die. When I finally did heal, despite my fear that I never would, I tried to forget it ever happened. It took a long time and when I met you, I discovered I was finally really and truly over the most traumatic experience in my life."

"But it's not over," she said in nearly a whisper. "Because she didn't have the abortion. She had the baby. Your baby." She swallowed.

He stood up. "I've got to see Carol. I have to see with my own eyes that she really is – my Carol. I can't believe it until I see her."

She didn't miss his reference to her as 'his' Carol. Did he still have feelings for her?

"I never stopped wondering what happened to her. Don't get me wrong; I'm not saying I think I still love her. I never loved her the way I love you. But at times, I've wondered how I would feel if she suddenly reappeared in my life."

Would he be as emotional as she'd been with Max? Or would it be even deeper for him, knowing that he and Carol had a child together, and that she hadn't left of her own accord, as Max had, but because her parents had given her no choice?

"I never knew she had the baby. Dani, I swear I thought she had the abortion. Her parents were adamant about it. Why didn't she let me know? If she couldn't tell me then, why didn't she contact me later on? I would have helped her. I would have sent her money. I would never have deserted and abandoned my child!"

Would he have married her? When he saw Carol again, would he discover he'd never stopped loving her after all? She remembered that Carol was quite possibly dying. Would that increase any sense of responsibility he felt for her?

THIRTY-TWO

THE PHONE WAS RINGING when Dani went inside and she wasn't surprised to hear Granny Jane's voice. Why had she left so suddenly? Was she all right?

Dani couldn't lie to her but neither could she tell her the truth. She simply commented that something unexpected had come up and she had to take care of it right away.

It made her feel better when Granny Jane promised to be praying for her and her new problem.

She and James decided it would be best to wait until the next day to visit Carol. They needed a little time to think about what had happened and pray about the right way to handle it.

The next morning, they drove back to the trailer court. As they got out of the car in front of Carol's house, Dani wasn't surprised to find herself trembling. What was going to happen when James and Carol saw each other again? Never in her life had she been so afraid. She and James were going to have their own child. Would he stay with her because of that? Or would he choose Carol and Star instead? She had no doubt he'd always take care of her and that he'd love their child and be there for it, but how could she ever be happy again without him in her life?

Despite his continual assurance that she was the one he loved, she couldn't shake the fears in her heart.

It was surprising to her when her mind reverted unexpectedly to Adam and Eve. Had they ever had any heartbreaking problems such as the one she was facing?

Why would she think of them at a time like this? And why would she need to wonder whether they'd been through heartbreak? Of course, they had. Their son killed his brother. Wasn't that a certain reason for pain and suffering?

"Because of our sin, the entire world will suffer. Because we chose to do what was forbidden, all future generations will face pain and heartache. But through it all, God will be there for them, just as He's always been here with us. All they have to do is believe in Him, love Him and trust Him, and when they do that, truly, all things will work together for their good."

She heard the words so clearly in her mind, almost as if the first man and woman were right there with her, speaking directly to her. A smile crossed her lips. She had to trust God with this big problem, just as she trusted Him with all the small ones. Even though it seemed like nothing she had ever experienced in her life had been as big as what she was now facing, wasn't God bigger than anything else imaginable?

James leaned over and kissed her lightly before they got out of the car. "I love you," he said. "I will always love you."

"I love you, too."

"Are you ready for this?"

"Yes."

Star met them on the walkway. It was almost as if she'd been expecting them and was waiting for them.

"Hello, Star," Dani said, smiling.

Star didn't smile. "I figured you'd be back. I just want you to know I haven't told Mom anything." Her eyes turned to

James. "It's your ballgame now. You explain to her why you did what you did all those years ago." She turned away then and walked to the door, opened it and said, "There's – someone here to see you, Mom." Then she left them alone and started quickly down the sidewalk.

Carol appeared in the doorway just as they stepped onto the porch. "Dani! I'm so glad you came back. I've been worried about you. This must be your hus……" She stopped mid-sentence when she looked up and saw James.

Their gazes locked as a hollow, deathly silence ensued.

Dani looked at Carol, then at James. Her husband's eyes were filled with tears and his body was jerking. His entire countenance was paler than she'd ever seen him. "Carol…."

She swallowed. "James. How? Why?"

Reaching out, he took Carol's hand. "I never knew," he said, his voice choking. "Honest to God, I never knew we had a daughter."

Carol said softly, "Let's go inside."

Once they were all seated, no one spoke. Dani looked at James and he looked at her. They both looked at Carol. Carol looked at Dani, then at James.

Then Carol spoke softly. "You have nothing to be sorry for, James. It was my decision not to contact you. After Star was born, I wanted to, but my parents convinced me not to. They reminded me over and over of my promise, that if they didn't make me have the abortion, I would never let you know about the baby. If I went against their wishes, they could still force me to put her up for adoption – and have you arrested for statutory rape. You see, I wasn't 17, like I told you. I was only 15."

He didn't speak.

"How did you find me? Was it Star? It was, wasn't it? That's why she's been so hateful to Dani, because she knew who you both were."

"Star told me yesterday that James was her biological father," Dani said. "That's why – I left so quickly. You see, we always thought you'd had the abortion, and of course, I had no idea who either of you were until she told me." There was no need to mention the fact that she'd never known they even existed until the day before.

"I don't know how Star found you," Carol then said. "But I know why. She's grown up hating you, James. In her childhood years, her grandparents told her stories about how you left because you didn't love either her or me and you didn't want the responsibility of us. I never knew any of this until they died and Star threw it in my face as a total surprise. I would've stopped it, if I'd known what they were doing. By the time I found out, Star was nearly ten years old, with a mind of her own and she wouldn't believe anything I said. She kept becoming more and more despondent.   I took her to counsellors that did nothing to help her. I never would've guessed that she hated you so much she was determined to find you and – somehow hurt you the way she thought you hurt her – and me."

"In all these years, why didn't you get in touch with me, Carol? I know you couldn't when you were younger, but you could have done so later. I would have helped you. I would have supported you."

"All I ever wanted was for you to be happy. By the time I was old enough to make my own decisions, I was already married. It was too late for us and I saw no reason to mess up your life again. I did all right. As I said, I married and had another daughter. Even though Joe didn't have much patience with the girls, I loved him and I believe he loved me. In his own way, he cared for the girls, too. He provided for us and we had all we needed. I remarried when he died. Jerry loved me and I loved him desperately, maybe even more than I thought I loved you, James, or than I loved Joe Light, but then he wanted nothing to do with me when I was diagnosed with terminal cancer. It's been a year since I've seen him."

"Carol, I'm so sorry!"

"Please stop saying that! I don't want you back in my life just to feel sorry for me."

There was a moment of silence, broken only by the opening of the door and the entrance of Star. Looking from one to another, her eyes finally stopped on her mother. "I went to see Granny Jane."

Everyone waited.

Star didn't look at any of them, but at the floor. "I've always been able to talk to Granny Jane but I never told her anything about my past. Today, I told her everything. I rattled on so fast that I was sure she didn't understand a word of what I was saying, but when I was done, she told me it didn't matter who my earthly father was, that even the best one on earth was only human and would wind up hurting me at some time or another. She said the only real father anybody ever has is God and that He's the only one who will ever love us unconditionally."

She lifted her eyes and turned them on Dani. "She told me how much she loves you, how good you've been to her, and how much you love your husband and the baby you're going to have. I – didn't know about the baby."

She shifted her gaze to James. "She told me that she saw something really special in you the first time she met you. She said you were a good man and she knew beyond the shadow of a doubt, that if you had known about me, you would have – you would have loved me and taken care of me." Her voice broke and she looked away from him.

No one spoke.

Star looked at her mother. "Granny Jane said the only reason you're fighting this cancer is because of me and Heaven, because you don't want to leave us. She said she knows that you love us so much that everything you ever did was – because you thought it was best for us. Everything, from the time we were born." She lowered her eyes and started crying.

It was James who stood up and went to her. Without a word, he put his arms around her and held her. She didn't move away or say a word. All either of them did was stand there for several moments – until Star opened her arms and put them around him.

"I wasn't there for you then," he told her, "but I am now. Dani and I are both here for you and for your mother and for your sister. Please give us a chance to share your lives, from this moment on."

She pulled away, looked at him and smiled.

It was the first time Dani had seen her smile and she couldn't help thinking how beautiful she was. As she watched her, she felt Star's eyes moving to her.

"I'm sorry," she said very softly.

Dani stood up, then helped Carol to her feet as well. Together, they walked over to James and Star and were soon all bound together in a group hug.

The door opened and closed and soon they all heard Granny Jane's excited laughter.

"I knew it!" she cried, her voice filled with delight. "I just knew it was going to be okay."

Star looked at the old lady. "How did you know?"

Another voice, an unexpected one, spoke from behind Granny Jane. "The same way I did."

Carol gasped. "Jerry!"

Star cried out. "Dad!"

Mr. Gordon stepped into the room. "I'm so sorry, Carol. And Star. I've been a fool. Granny Jane's been talking to me lately. Don't ask me how we got together. It's a long story. But the moral of it is, God got hold of me and showed me the error of my ways, through Granny Jane, no doubt, and I want my family back, if you'll have me."

Everyone watched as Carol ran to her husband and fell into his embrace.

"I heard what you said," he told her. "No one knew I'd been standing at the back door listening, while Star was with Granny Jane. Do you really love me the best?"

"I really do!"

"We're going to beat this cancer," he told her. "Together, with God's help, we're going to get you well."

Star smiled, a smile that lit her entire countenance. "I spent my whole life angry because I wanted a father that I never believed wanted me," she said. "While I was wasting all those years brooding and wanting revenge, my real Father,

God, was trying to work everything out for me but I refused to let Him. He was a forbidden part of my life because I blamed Him for everything and refused to have anything to do with Him. And all along, He knew that James would love me if he knew about me. He knew that Jerry really cared but just needed time to find himself. He even knew that Joe cared and he wasn't nearly as bad as I'd made him out to be. Do you all know what I'm trying to say? I have had, not just one, but three earthly fathers, as well as one loving and caring Heavenly Father – and they all loved me! How lucky can one person be?"

Granny Jane laughed. "Luck has nothing to do with it, child. The destiny of every one of us started years and years ago, in a place where there was nothing but eerie darkness and deathly silence everywhere – in every corner, every nook and crevice and every inch of space – until God saw the possibility of hope in the midst of nothingness……"

And then God made man and breathed the breath of life into him, Dani thought, smiling. He gave him everything, except permission to eat that one forbidden fruit, but when he disobeyed, God still kept loving him. Just as He was still loving every single person in the world.

THE END

NOTE FROM THE AUTHOR

Thank you so much for reading FORBIDDEN.
I hope you've enjoyed it and would appreciate it so much if
you would leave a review on www.amazon.com.

Please see the next page for a list of my other books, all of
which can be previewed and/or ordered on
www.joanfennellcarringer.com and www.amazon.com.

GOD BLESS YOU!

INSPIRATIONAL FICTION BOOKS
<u>BY Joan Fennell Carringer</u>

In the Midst of Tomorrow
Touching a Dream
Shattered Yesterdays
Forbidden
<u>ILLUSTRATED CHILDREN</u>
Angels Beside the Children (Vol. I & II)

<u>ANGEL JACK BOOKS</u>
Listed in sequence but can be read in any order.

#1 - Walking with an Angel

#2 - Crossing the Shadows

#3 - It Only Takes One

#4 - Tears of an Angel

#5 - Beyond Chance

#6 - IF ONLY

#7 – The Doorway of Forever

#8 – Always an Angel

#9 - Dusty Clouds

#10 - Between Now and Then

#11 - Angel Baby

<u>INSPIRATIONAL SCI-FICTION</u>
Planet Mystic Series: Stand alone but best when read in order.

#1 -The Mystical Challenge

#2 - The Love Emotion

#3 - Princess on Probation

#4 – Mystic

#5 –The Dream Trip

#6 – Guardian Angel

#7 – The Mystical Secret: Up for Bids!

All books can be previewed at:
www.joanfennellcarringer.com

The following are scriptures referred to in FORBIDDEN.
All are taken from the King James Version of The Holy Bible.

CHAPTER ONE

In the beginning, God created the heaven and the earth. And the earth was without form, and void; and darkness was upon the face of the deep. And the Spirit of God moved upon the face of the waters. – Genesis 1:1,2

Before the mountains were brought forth, or ever thou hadst formed the earth and the world, even from everlasting to everlasting, thou art God. – Psalm 90:2

In the beginning was the Word, and the Word was with God, and the Word was God. The same was in the beginning with God. All things were made by him; and without him was not anything made that was made. In him was life; and the life was the light of men. – John 1:1-427

And the Lord God formed man of the dust of the ground, and breathed into his nostrils the breath of life, and man became a living soul. – Genesis 2:7

So God created man in his own image, in the image of God created he him; male and female created he them. – Genesis 1:27.

Let every soul be subject unto the higher powers. For there is no power but of God: the powers that be are ordained of God. – Romans 13:1

And the Lord God said, It is not good that the man should be alone; I will make him an help meet for him. – Genesis 2:18

And the Lord God caused a deep sleep to fall upon Adam, and he slept; and He took one of his ribs, and closed up the flesh instead thereof: And the rib, which the Lord God had taken from the man, made he a woman, and brought her unto the man. And Adam said, This is now bone of my bones, and flesh of my flesh; she shall be called Woman, because she was taken out of Man. – Genesis 2:21-23

And Adam called his wife's name Eve, because she was the mother of all living. – Genesis 3:20

CHAPTER TWO

Read Genesis, Chapter Three.

CHAPTER SIX

Ye shall know the truth and the truth shall make you free. – John 8:32

CHAPTER NINETEEN

There is no fear in love; but perfect love casteth out fear: because fear hath torment. He that feareth is not made perfect in love. - 1 John 4:8

Ye shall not fear them: for the Lord your God he shall fight for you. - Deut. 3:22

And he saith unto them, Why are ye fearful, O ye of little faith? Then he arose, and rebuked the winds and the sea; and there was a great calm. - Matt. 8:26

For God hath not given us the spirit of fear; but of power, and of love, and of a sound mind. - II Tim 1:7

Lord, I believe; help thou mine unbelief. – Mark 9:24

CHAPTER TWENTY-ONE

And we know that all things work together for good to them that love God, to them who are the called according to his purpose. – Romans 8:28 (Also in Chapter 28).

CHAPTER TWENTY-TWO

For if ye forgive men their trespasses, your heavenly father will also forgive you. But if ye forgive not men their trespasses, neither will your father forgive your trespasses – Matthew 6:14-15

CHAPTER TWENTY-EIGHT

For ye have need of patience, that, after ye have done the will of God, ye might receive the promise. – Hebrews 10:36